The Angels

of

Lockhart

Thom L. Wiley

The Parker Family, Circ. 1915

The Angels
of
Lockhart

By
Thomas L. Wiley

Cover and author photo by Merrie Wiley

Monarch Publishing House
2573 Lake Circle
Jackson, MS 39211-6630

Copyright © 2007, Thomas Wiley

ISBN: 978-0-9797861-0-5

Library of Congress Control Number: 2007931558

Printed in the United States of America

This book is dedicated
to
Tom

The Introduction

In rural Mississippi, ten miles north of Meridian, there is an old
church cemetery where seven babies, all brothers and sisters,
are buried in a lonely, nearly forgotten family plot. For years, my
wife, Merrie, had talked about Lockhart Cemetery and her step-
great-grandmother, Lizzie Parker, who, from 1890 to 1910,
buried all seven of her children. According to the family, these little ones died of common childhood illnesses—victims of diseases
that are now rarely fatal, born in a time when medicine had very
little to offer. But has the truth about these children really been
told? Were these deaths as innocent as the family would have us
believe, or is there more to the story of the Angels of Lockhart
Cemetery?

I had never paid much attention to the story of Lizzie and her
babies until one January day when Merrie and I made an afternoon trip to Meridian to check on her father's ten-year-old grave.
After visiting Magnolia Cemetery, we still had plenty of time before dark and were in no big hurry to get back to Jackson. Merrie
suggested that we drive to Lockhart and check on those graves,

too. Never could I have imagined how our visit on that beautiful winter day would haunt me the way it has.

Lockhart is a little community, or at least used to be a community, ten miles north of Meridian on Highway 45. In 1895, it boasted a post office, a railroad depot, and one hundred residents. The town has long since disappeared and the only thing remaining there is the Lockhart Methodist Church and its cemetery.

Meridian's history is different. In 1854, when the railroad was rapidly replacing the river as the preferred mode of transporting goods and people, the Mobile & Ohio Railway (running north and south) intersected the Alabama & Vicksburg Railroad (east and west) in central Mississippi near the Alabama border. Thus Meridian was born, and being the main railway intersection in the state, the town grew quickly. In 1860, it was incorporated and in 1900, had 25,000 citizens. From 1890 until 1930, "the Queen City," as she was affectionately known, was the largest city in the state, and even today continues to be a thriving metropolis of nearly 40,000.

It had been several years since Merrie had been to the cemetery in Lockhart, and this was my first visit. Buried there is Merrie's *real* great-grandmother, Georgia S. Perkins Parker, alongside the seven babies of her *step*-great-grandmother.

The story of the Parker family began in 1876 when, at age sixteen, Georgia married twenty-three year old Stephen Decatur Parker and bore him four children before dying in 1886 at age twenty-six. Shortly before her death, one of their children had died, leaving Stephen, now thirty-two, with three little ones to rear. Two years later, Stephen remarried. His nineteen year old bride was Elizabeth (Lizzie) Josephine Bludworth.

Merrie told me how her step-great-grandmother, Lizzie, while rearing three children not her own, started having babies one after another—seven of them. But not a single one would live beyond childhood. All would die. None of her natural-born children would live to see their promised future unfold. All of them would be buried in a sad little row in Lockhart Cemetery, alongside Stephen's first wife. According to Merrie's father, they died of diseases that are now cured with just a few days of pills, or totally prevented by immunizations.

Merrie also said that she had an old photo somewhere, made in 1951, with Lizzie holding her when she was six weeks old. Lizzie died four months later at age eighty-three.

As we drove north from Meridian on Highway 45 toward Lockhart, Merrie remarked how the highway had changed. The last time she was there she was able to see the church and cemetery from the highway, but now the trees and brush had taken over. She told me to look for Minnow Bucket Road. As if on cue, the old road sign "Minnow Bucket Road" appeared.

We pulled off the highway and there was the church: "Lockhart Methodist Church, Established 1885." It was obvious that the church had not been used in quite some time. The only doors, located at the rear of the church, were locked shut, and the old padlock was rusty. The windows were too high off the ground to peer in, but the doors were warped and didn't close well. There was just enough space between them to get a glimpse of the inside. The neat rows of pews were dusty and the floor littered with dead wasps and dirt dauber nests. The church was a small one room building, approximately forty feet square, and would seat maybe seventy-five people.

The outside of the church was fairly well-maintained. The foundation had been worked on sometime in the past few years with new brick and mortar. The white paint on the church, though starting to peel, didn't appear to be but a few years old. The roof was in pretty good shape for a church well over one hundred and twenty years old.

Directly behind the old church was the cemetery. It was about two hundred feet by three hundred feet, the short side of the rectangle being along the back of the church. Like the church, it was also well-maintained. The iron fence and gates were painted silver, with just a little rust showing here and there. The grass appeared to have been cut on a regular basis and few weeds were present around the fence and gravestones, evidence that someone really took care of this old place. Looking around, there were approximately four hundred stones and markers, dating from the 1880's to the 1990's.

Near the middle of the cemetery was the Parker family plot; it was rectangular, approximately twenty feet by thirty-five feet, surrounded by a concrete border. There were twelve gravestones arranged in two rows—three graves on the top row and eight on the bottom row, and a tiny marker between the rows to the left. The stones were the usual rough gray granite that was typical of that era. They were fairly worn by the elements but could be read without much difficulty.

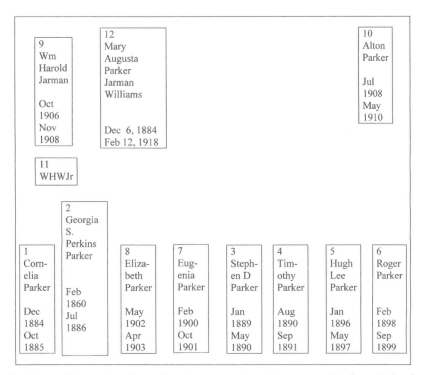

(To keep things simple and easier to read, only names, birth and death dates are given here. See Appendix A for the complete writings on each headstone. The number in the left upper corner of each marker gives the order of burial.)

As I looked at the stone markers, I found it interesting to see the burial sequence in this little family plot. The first to be buried was Cornelia, a daughter of Stephen and Georgia, who died in 1885 at eleven months of age. Next to be laid to rest was Georgia, Stephen's wife, who died at age twenty-six in 1886. Four years later, in 1890, the first of the seven babies of Stephen and his second wife, Lizzie, was buried: fifteen month old "baby" Stephen. (Notice that there were two spaces left between Georgia and this baby, apparently to be the final resting place for Stephen and Lizzie.) The next three babies, Timothy, Hugh, and Roger, were laid to rest next to their brother, Stephen, in their sequence of death, at ages twelve months, sixteen months, and nineteen months.

Following the four little boys were two little girls, Eugenia, at twenty months, and Elizabeth at eleven months, both laid to rest between their father's first wife, Georgia, and "baby" Stephen, in the plots where I assume Stephen and Lizzie were to be buried. Apparently they ran out of room on the row, and Stephen and Lizzie must have decided by this time that they would be buried elsewhere.

In 1910, Alton, at twenty-two months, was the last of Stephen and Lizzie's seven children to die. With no more room on the lower row, he was placed by himself in the upper right corner of the family plot. Almost twenty years had passed from the death of the first of the seven siblings to the death of the last.

Up until the past seventy-five years, death of a child was an all too common occurrence. Visit any old family cemetery, and among the gravestones you will almost always find at least one tiny stone—a permanent reminder of a child who once was loved and cherished but now unknown and forgotten. Families understood that the chances of all of their children reaching adulthood were very low; one or two would often succumb to the ravages of childhood diseases and epidemics. Families were big partly because more hands were needed to work and survive, but also because death of some was almost certain to occur.

Things changed in the mid twentieth century. In 1938, penicillin was discovered, a wonder drug that was a miracle cure for bacterial infections like strep throat and its common sequella, rheumatic fever. Other more powerful and broad spectrum antibiotics would be discovered that would make most bacterial infections a mere nuisance. Also, the widespread acceptance of immunizations would make many scourges of the past, such as whooping cough, diphtheria, and polio, almost disappear from society. No longer would a fever, a cough, or a sore throat strike fear in the hearts of young parents. A simple visit to the doctor, or only a phone call, would turn death away. The United States and other industrialized countries would see the leading cause of child mortality change from infections to congenital anomalies: not because there are more anomalies, but because so few children die of infections.

As I was looking at the little stones, it suddenly hit me that something wasn't right. Something didn't fit. Here were seven babies who all died between the ages of eleven months and twenty-two months. Each had died before the next one was born. There was no epidemic that had come through the community and wiped out the future of Stephen's second family. No two deaths were related; each loss a loss unto itself. There was no history in the family of any genetic or inherited diseases that would have led to infant death, and as far as anyone knew, each child had been a healthy, normal baby.

It may have been my imagination, but I felt a sudden breeze blow through the cemetery and a cold, haunting shiver came over me as I stood there looking at those little markers. What went on in this family one hundred years ago? Were these deaths only bad luck for this poor family or had something dark and evil been buried there so long ago? Was this the result of Death's innocent but harsh visit, or had Death been an invited guest? Have these deaths ever raised any suspicion at all, either to the family and friends of a century ago, or to the children and grandchildren who would visit? Had anyone in the past had the same thoughts that I was having? Are there any answers?

Sadly, the players in this story have long been erased by time. Stephen Parker died in the 1930's and his wife, Lizzie, step-mother to three, but mother to only babies, lived until 1952, dying at age eighty-three. Her step-children, all born in the 1880's, have been dead for years. As far as we know, there is nothing written about the lives of the Parker family in Lockhart, Mississippi.

As we walked away from that sad, forgotten cemetery, I looked back at those seven tiny graves, the Angels of Lockhart Cemetery, and thought, whatever the circumstances, how heartbreaking for the Parker family of a hundred years ago . . . And the answers? The answers were buried long ago, hidden forever, never to be unearthed. And maybe that is for the best.

For weeks after our visit to the Lockhart Cemetery, I could not stop thinking about those babies, their lives and their deaths, and wondering, is this all there is? Is there more to the Parker family and the deaths of their babies? Were terrible, tragic secrets taken to their graves so long ago? What is the truth, and can the truth be pieced together?

This story, like so many true stories of the past, is filled with blanks and gaps that will never be filled; we are just left to wonder. However, imagination can come along and take a few facts and create a story where all the "facts" are known. The rest of this book is just that: a story where some of the "facts" are imaginary. The names, places, and dates, for the most part, are real, but the thoughts, ideas, actions, and day-to-day activities are not.

I have tried to make the story and characters as authentic and real as possible, recognizing that there are limitations due to the passage of time. Through interviews with relatives and through tales of the family that my wife could remember, I was able to get to know the Parker family of one hundred years ago rather well. I was able to learn their personalities and their little quirks. Also, through research of census reports, birth certificates, death certificates, marriage licenses, and multiple trips to Meridian, the Lockhart community, and the Mississippi Archives, I was able to piece together a fairly authentic timeline. What follows is a story of what had to have been a truly heartbreaking chapter in the life of this poor family.

The Angels
of
Lockhart

By
Thomas L. Wiley

Chapter 1

January 21, 1952
Magnolia Cemetery
Meridian, Mississippi

Today we buried my stepmother, Elizabeth Parker—"Lizzie" to family and friends. The quiet graveside service gave no hint of the sorrow, the grief, and the suspicion that gripped our family over forty years ago. As we stood beside the grave, my heart ached; not because of her death, but because of memories of seven babies: my half brothers and sisters, buried long ago in Lockhart Cemetery.

The Reverend James looked down at his notes as he started the eulogy: "We are gathered here to celebrate the life and the heavenly home-going of Elizabeth Bludworth Parker. She was born eighty-three years ago on March 16, 1868, and died two days ago, January 19, 1952. She was the daughter of T. W. and Charlotte Bludworth, and was the loving wife of Stephen Decatur Parker, who preceded her in death twenty-one years ago."

Has it really been twenty-one years since Papa died? The time has passed so quickly. It seems only yesterday that we laid him to rest here in Magnolia Cemetery. I had wanted to bury him in Lockhart in the Parker family plot with the rest of the family, but

Lizzie would not agree. She said that she wanted him here, not ten miles away, so that she could come and put flowers on his grave. But the truth, I believe, is that she did not want to ever return to the Lockhart Cemetery. To my knowledge, she has not stepped foot in that cemetery since the last of her seven children was buried there over forty years ago. In fact, I don't think she has even been to Lockhart since then.

The Reverend cleared his throat and continued, "Jesus said, 'I am the resurrection and the life. He that believeth in me, though he were dead, yet shall he live, and whosoever liveth and believeth in me, shall never die.'"

Lockhart: the little community where I was born and where I lived the first twenty-four years of my life. A place filled with memories, both wonderful and tragic.

"We brought nothing into this world, and it is certain we can carry nothing out." The Reverend paused and looked up from his notes. "The Lord giveth, and the Lord taketh away; blessed be the name of the Lord."

Seven babies. All of her children buried in a sad row in Lockhart Cemetery, buried beside *my* mother. And here in Meridian, *their* mother and *our* father are buried among strangers! I still can't understand it. Lizzie wanted no part in the memory of those little angels, not even in death. For the past forty years it has been as if the twenty years before that, the twenty years of having babies and watching them die, did not even exist.

"Behold, I show you a mystery." The Reverend James adjusted his glasses. "We shall not all sleep, but we shall all be changed, in a moment, in the twinkling of an eye, at the last trump; for the trumpet shall sound, and the dead shall be raised incorruptible, and we shall be changed . . . Death is swallowed up in victory. O Death, where is thy sting? O Grave, where is thy victory? . . . But thanks be to God, which giveth us the victory through our Lord Jesus Christ."

Forty years of silence. Only in the past two or three years had she begun to speak of her little angels. And it seems that recently, as her mind and health began to fail, she became obsessed with their lives and deaths; nothing else seemed to be on her mind. Only a few months ago, while my nephew, Arthur, and his family were visiting, Lizzie spoke more about those babies than I had heard her speak in years.

I remember Lizzie rocking Arthur's six-week-old daughter and saying, "Ollie, isn't Merrie a beautiful baby? She looks a lot like Stephen did. You remember him, don't you? He was my first born, a beautiful little boy. When he got sick and died, I felt like the world had come to an end. I just wanted to die, too.

"And then Timothy. Ollie, you remember Timothy, too, don't you? He was my second child. When he died, again I wanted to die with my baby.

"After Timothy, there was Hugh, and Roger, then my two precious girls, Eugenia and Elizabeth, and the last one was Alton. All of them. Beautiful little angels, all gone. All buried in Lockhart Cemetery.

"It got to where I knew they wouldn't last. Like God had cursed me, never to see my babies grow up. It was so hard to love when I expected death to come. And, Ollie, I still hurt so badly when I think about my little babies. Time, even forty years, hasn't taken away the pain."

I remember Lizzie held Arthur's baby close and she began to cry.

"Man, that is born of a woman, hath but a short time to live, and is full of misery. He cometh up, and is cut down, like a flower; he fleeth as it were a shadow, and never continueth in one stay." The Reverend paused and looked up toward the sky. "Yet, O Lord God most holy, O Lord most mighty, O holy and most merciful Savior, deliver us not into the bitter pains of eternal death."

How did our family bear so much pain and heartache? And even worse, how did we bear the suspicion and mistrust that ultimately consumed us?

"Family and friends," the Reverend James said as he closed his Book, "let us be comforted with these words of hope spoken by our Lord Jesus, 'Let not your heart be troubled; ye believe in God, believe also in Me. In my father's house are many mansions; if it were not so, I would have told you. I go to prepare a place for you. And . . . I will come again, and receive you unto myself; that where I am, there ye may be also.'"

Lizzie is now gone, and this chapter in the life of my family closes. But to this day, I still wonder about the deaths of my little brothers and sisters. And with her death, the truth may have also died; we may never know what really happened to those babies.

And now, let me tell you the story of my family and the Angels of Lockhart.

Chapter 2

Sixty-five years ago, my mother, Georgia S. Perkins Parker, died at the age of twenty-six. The year was 1886. I was only eight years old, but I remember those times so well. We were very close, my mother and I, and when she died, I truly think a part of me died with her. I often think back on those days long ago when we would sit and talk, just the two of us, about all the wonderful things in this world that would interest an eight-year-old boy. She was young and beautiful, and she had the gift of warmth, love, and kindness.

There were also Maude and Gussie, my four-year-old and eighteen-month-old sisters; but in my mind I was the only child. Never did I feel that I was sharing my mother with anyone. At least that is the way I remember those times. In those memories of so long ago, or maybe in my imagination, I remember her whispering as I would drift off to sleep that she loved me more than anything else in the world.

Mama loved to tell me stories about when she and Papa met and when they married. She was only sixteen years old when she left home. Her mother had died when she was fourteen and her father had remarried quickly, mainly to have someone take care of the children. Being the oldest, at first Mama was glad to no longer be the caregiver to her two siblings; but she quickly learned that her new mother wanted her out. She brought with her two teenage daughters, and there was not enough room for the three of them.

Their home town, Lockhart, was a small farming community with a much smaller general store. So every few weeks my grandfather would make the ten-mile trip to Meridian to buy supplies. Meridian had been on the map for only twenty years, but, because of the railroad, had already become a booming little city. On his trips to the city he would often have anywhere from one to five children in tow.

One spring Saturday morning in 1876, it was only he and my mother, sixteen-year-old Georgia, making the two and a half hour wagon ride. It was on this day that she met Stephen Decatur Parker, a tall likeable twenty-three year old gentleman who was working in one of the general stores in Meridian. Mama said he had a smile that would melt your heart. I barely remember that smile, because after Mama died, his smile was never the same. She told me how on that first meeting, she knew he was the one who would be her husband. Before long my father was making weekly Sunday afternoon trips to Lockhart to visit this young beauty, and within a few months asked for her hand. Everyone was happy, especially the stepmother.

Mama told me all about Papa's family, the Parkers, who were originally from Lockhart but had moved away when she was five years old. At one time the Parkers had been one of the most prominent families in the Lockhart community. Papa's father, John Woods Parker, had owned one of the largest plantations in the area, but the Civil War came and they lost everything. With nothing left for them in Lockhart, the Parkers moved to Meridian. Papa was twelve years old at the time and, at twenty-three, he still considered Lockhart his hometown. Mama said that he had always wanted to come back to Lockhart to live.

Papa and Mama married and settled in Lockhart. The year was 1876, and over the next ten years they lived a life of love and happiness.

When Papa arrived in Lockhart, he had no job and very little money, but he soon found work at the general store. The old store had been owned and operated by John Hill for as long as anyone could remember and was a fairly busy little enterprise. Mr. Hill was getting on in years, and it soon became obvious to Papa that Mr. Hill's sons were not interested in carrying on the family business.

After working at the general store for a few months, Papa made Mr. Hill a generous offer for the business and was able to secure a loan from one of the banks in Meridian. Papa was soon the proud owner of the Lockhart General Store. Old Mr. Hill retired and he and his wife, Clelia, were able to live comfortably until their deaths a decade later.

One of the first things Papa did with the general store was to make it into two stores. The original general store was a typical old country store with everything stocked everywhere. You might find axle grease on the same shelf as castor oil, or flour next to chicken feed. Papa purchased a tract of land across the road from the original store, and in no time erected a new building. He turned the old store into a farming supply store and the new one into a household goods store which provided items such as sewing supplies, clothing, housewares, and food staples. Everyone in our little community was impressed. The women could shop in their store and the men in theirs. Before long, Papa was making a very respectable living in the little town of Lockhart.

Through the years Papa became known as a very clever businessman and had a knack for making good, honest deals where everyone involved came out feeling like a winner.

Mama and Papa had four children. I was the first, born in 1877. They named me Oliver, but everyone called me Ollie. Four years later came Maude. In another two years there was a happy surprise: twins, Mary Augusta "Gussie" and Cornelia Jewel, both healthy, happy little babies. Life was busy for our family, but life was good. Everything seemed so perfect.

But sadness came to visit: one of the twins, little Cornelia, died at eleven months from a fever. Six months later Mama died. She was pregnant again, and a few months before the baby was due, she began having severe headaches that would not go away. One morning Papa found her on the floor having convulsions. Dr. Knox was called. He said that Mama had developed "toxemia," and there was nothing he could do. She never woke up after the convulsions, and she and her unborn child died that night. She was buried in Lockhart Cemetery, where over the next twenty years our family would bury many more little angels.

When Mama died, Papa was left to care for three young children. He tried his best to be both father and mother, but he just couldn't do everything that was needed. I remember how hard it was; the house was so sad and lonely during those times.

To the rescue came Mamaw Parker, Papa's mother. Four years earlier my grandfather had died, and Mamaw was left alone in Meridian. She was more than happy to move back to Lockhart and take care of us. She was just what our grieving family needed and soon filled the void of mother and caregiver. She and I developed a closeness, a bond, which lasted until she died twenty years later.

Mamaw was short and almost as round as she was tall. Arthritis had affected her hips and when she walked, she almost waddled. But she didn't let it affect her. She was a wonderful, happy lady and was never without a smile. Mamaw was also a wonderful listener. When I would take my troubles to her, she would listen intently and have just the right answer that would make the world right again.

For another year and a half, things settled down and the family went about the business of living. Papa went to work and

Mamaw took care of the household duties. The girls did what little girls do, and I tried to get along without Mama. Soon Maude and Gussie had very little memory of our beautiful, loving mother, but I continued to miss her. Sometimes when I would watch them playing and having a good time, with not a sad memory in their little heads, I would wonder who was better off. Was it better to have no memory of one you loved and who loved you dearly, or was it better to have the memories but also have the pain? Looking back now, I will take the memories and the pain.

But things were soon to change. A little over a year after Mama died, Papa met Elizabeth Josephine Bludworth—"Lizzie." In fact, we all met her together one Sunday morning in July. She and her family had just moved to Lockhart from Tennessee and were settling into the community. Part of the "settling in" ritual in the South is finding a church. On that particular Sunday morning we were all sitting on the pew in front of her family: Lizzie; her mother and father, T. W. and Charlotte; her five brothers, James, John, Timothy, Thomas, and Junius; and her sister, Lottie. (I've often wondered where they came up with Junius. One would expect Peter or Paul, but Junius?) Papa introduced himself and us to the newcomers, and Mamaw, being a gracious neighbor, invited them to join us for Sunday dinner.

I remember Mrs. Bludworth thanking Mamaw and saying that she and her family would be glad to join us, but that adding nine hungry mouths to anyone's table would be a strain. She said she already had a chicken in the oven and some sweet corn shucked and ready to boil, and that she and her girls would run by the house, bring it over, and add it to our table.

It was a great afternoon. In Mississippi, Sunday afternoons are for eating, visiting, and resting, and we did all three. In July it's usually too hot and muggy to do much else. After dinner, the adults settled in to visit and I took two of Lizzie's brothers, James and

Junius, who were about my age, down to the pond for a swim. We hit it off, and Junius, James, and I became best buddies. In fact, we remained close throughout the years, even after we had all moved from "Little Lockhart," as we used to call our tiny community.

When we got back to the house, Mamaw and Lizzie's parents were on the porch having a nice visit. Papa and Lizzie had gone for a walk and were not back yet. Lizzie's sister, Lottie, was sitting on the front steps, crocheting.

Lottie was "a little different." She was pleasant and smiled most of the time, but she rarely said anything. She never went to school and was never seen without her mother, always following her around like a puppy. Junius later told me that Lottie was "different" because their mother had been scared by a snake before she was born, but Mamaw said it was because Charlotte had been in labor too long. Interestingly, Lottie could crochet, and her work was flawless—no errors, no missed stitches. She spent almost every waking hour with hook and yarn in hand, making all types of pretty, lacey things. Show her any design and in no time she would have an exact copy that was often more beautiful than the original.

The other Bludworth boys, John, Timothy, and Thomas, who were a bit older, had gone home. James and Junius wanted to stay and play, so I pulled out my bag of marbles and we played "Ringer" for awhile.

When Papa and Lizzie returned, I remember noticing that Papa was different. A little bit of the sadness that seemed to hang over him had disappeared. As a nine year old, it didn't strike me that something might be developing between Papa and Lizzie. But over the next few weeks he began to visit her regularly, and the sadness continued to disappear.

Soon, Lizzie began to spend time in our home. She acted like a mother to my sisters, helping them put on their fancy dresses and lacing up their shoes. Maude was five and Gussie was two and a half, and they fell in love with Lizzie; they would squeal every time she came to visit.

Lizzie was nineteen years old and Papa was thirty-four. Today that age difference seems a bit odd, but sixty years ago it was a very common and accepted practice for older, more established men to court younger women. Many more women died young than men at that time, primarily, as in our family's case, due to childbirth and its complications. Also since there were very few women who were not already married by the time they were in their thirties, and since divorce was almost unheard of, the "pool" of eligible brides for older widowers was young.

In early September, two months after Papa and Lizzie had started courting, Mamaw announced that she was moving out of the house. She said that she needed some space of her own, but quickly added that she wasn't leaving us and planned to continue all the duties she had been doing for the family. I was confused with her sudden decision to move, because Mamaw had her own room in our house and had all the privacy she could ever want. But in looking back now, I realize that she was preparing the way for a new woman of the house. Even though she and Lizzie got along very well, she knew that she needed to be out of the way.

There was a house just down the road from ours that had been vacant for the past two or three years, and Papa was able to purchase it for next to nothing. It was in fairly good shape with a roof that, surprisingly, did not leak. Mamaw moved in, and with a little help from Lizzie, was able to convert that old house into a beautiful little cottage. Over time that cottage became my haven, the place where I would go when things went wrong, when I felt that the weight of the world was on my shoulders, or when I just needed some encouragement from my wonderful, wise grandmother.

Then one Sunday afternoon in October, Papa gave us the news. He told us that we were going to have a new mother. He and Lizzie were to get married in November. The girls and Mamaw were elated, but it was like a dagger to my heart. Even though I knew their wedding was going to happen, hearing him say it was more than I could stand. I felt that my mother was being pushed aside, to be forgotten even more than she already was.

As with all my troubles and fears, I took my concerns to Mamaw.

Chapter 3

The next day after school I stopped by Mamaw's house like I did almost every afternoon, looking forward to a piece of apple pie. Mamaw was well-known throughout our little community for her cooking and her pies were exceptional! A better description may be legendary! The crust was so flaky and soft, and the filling was to die for. No matter what time of day I stopped by, there was always a pie in the oven, or at least that's how I remember my visits. Her little cottage was always filled with the sweet aroma of fresh baked delights.

In October, her specialty was warm apple pie, accompanied by a glass of cold milk. The apples at this time of the year were still fresh, not canned like the rest of the year, and she put just the right amount of cinnamon and sugar in her pies to keep a boy like me coming back day after day for a piece or two.

She was washing dishes when I walked in, but stopped everything when she heard the screen door creak open.

"How was school today?" she asked as she dried off her hands and pulled a pie from the pantry. "You look awfully deep in thought this afternoon."

"Mamaw, I don't want them to get married. We don't need her," I answered as I pulled up a chair, sat down, and took a bite of pie.

"Ollie, some day you will understand," she said as she poured me a glass of milk.

"Papa has everything he needs," I replied. "He's got Maude and Gussie and me. And he's got you to take care of us. Why can't he be happy with us?"

"That's not it at all," Mamaw said. "Your father is very happy with you and your sisters. He loves you very much, but he needs more. He needs a wife. In a few years you will see what I mean. A man needs to have someone to love, someone to share his thoughts and dreams with. God knew what he was doing when he made a help mate for Adam—someone who would be 'flesh of his flesh and bone of his bone'; an equal. God made Eve from his rib, from his side; a partner that Adam would hold close under his arm. A man's love for his children is great and wonderful, but his love for a woman is different."

"But, Mamaw, you've done just fine without Grandpa," I said as I took another bite of pie. "You get along just fine."

Mamaw paused a moment, took a deep breath, and softly sighed. "I do all right, most of the time, but I still miss him so. Besides, women tend to get along better than men when their mate is gone. Men either find someone soon or they mourn themselves to death. You want your father around for a while, don't you? You know it has been over a year since your mother died."

I stopped eating and looked up at Mamaw with tears in my eyes. "But how can Papa forget Mama so soon?"

"Oh, Ollie!" Mamaw exclaimed. "Your father hasn't forgotten your mother and he never will. He will always love her more than you will ever know."

She pulled up a chair beside me, sat down, and held both of my hands in hers. She smiled and said, "Your mother was his first love. I wish that you could have seen him when he came home that spring day and told me he had found the girl he would marry.

At sixteen, she made such a beautiful bride for your father. She made his life complete. And they were so happy together. No, Ollie, he will never forget her. She will always be in his heart. But she is gone. As much as we want it, she is not coming back. And life has to go on."

She patted me gently on the knee, and then stood up. She filled my glass with more milk and said, "Now finish up your pie and run on home. I'm sure you have some chores that need to be done before it gets dark. And remember," she continued, "your grandma isn't getting any younger. I love taking care of you and your sisters, but it's getting hard to keep up with you little Indians. At the end of the day I'm just flat worn out. You need a young mother."

"I don't need a new mother!" I shouted as I slammed my fork down on the table. "I had a mother and I don't want another one! She can never take her place!"

"You're right, Ollie. She will never take your mother's place. Your mother will always be your mother. You will remember her forever. But think about your sisters. You were eight when your mother died. But Maude was four and little Gussie was only a year and a half. They won't remember her and will never have those memories like you do. And they need a mother, someone to love as only girls and their mother can. They need someone to teach them how to be little ladies. I know that you want the best for your sisters. And Lizzie is so good with them. They already love her so."

I remember laying my head down on the table and sobbing, "Mamaw, I miss Mama so much."

Chapter 4

Papa and Lizzie were married in November 1887, and again life settled down. Papa had a loving wife, and Maude and Gussie had a wonderful mother. Lizzie and I developed a good relationship, but I never saw her as my mother. I just never could make it happen. I think part of the problem was that she was only nine years my senior. It was more like having an older sister in the house than a mother. In fact, Mamaw continued to be my confidant, the one with whom I would share my joys, and the one to whom I would pour out my soul.

Lizzie quickly settled into the wifely duties of caring for a ready-made family. She was a pleasant, tall young lady, with long wavy light brown hair that she allowed to flow unhindered while she was at home. However, as was the custom at that time, she would twist it into a tight "bun" on the back of her head whenever she was out and about town. She was an excellent cook and housekeeper, and things really didn't miss a beat without Mamaw there. Mamaw didn't disappear, though. She was in and out of our home almost every day helping with the girls and with chores. But she knew how to let Lizzie be in charge and be the lady of the house, and she and Lizzie became the best of friends.

Eventually, Lizzie and I became good friends, but it was more like a sister-brother relationship than a mother-son. She treated me as a young adult rather than a ten or eleven year old child. After all, we *were* only nine years apart in age.

Lizzie was a lot of fun to talk with and had a very keen sense of humor. Dinnertime was always an enjoyable time, with her and Papa making up little jokes and stories that would make us laugh. But there was always a little distance between us—a mutual understanding that she was not, and never would be, my mother.

The first winter that Lizzie was with us, 1887–1888, was exceptionally cold. If you know anything about central Mississippi, you know that a cold winter day is when the high doesn't get above fifty degrees. But this year we had two weeks in January where the temperature did not rise above freezing. And it snowed!—and not the little dusting that we would occasionally see.

In less than a week, two snowstorms blew through leaving four to six inches of snow each time. School didn't meet and Lizzie's brothers, Junius and James, and I had a field day! Behind our house was a fairly steep hill leading down to the pasture, and we improvised a sled using an old watering trough. We spent days flying down that slippery slope and dragging that heavy piece of metal back up. Going down, it was such a small hill, but climbing back up it was a mountain! Even Maude, Gussie, and Lizzie joined in the fun. Lizzie was like one of us kids during those cold wintry days and, like the girls, seemed to not have a care in the world. Papa would stand at the top of the hill and laugh until he could laugh no more as we flew down the hill.

But over the next few years, I would see the innocence and the happiness in Lizzie and Papa slowly fade away.

In May of 1888, a change came over Lizzie. She was sick almost every morning and didn't seem to have the energy to get the chores done around the house like she had been. Instead of Lizzie,

Mamaw would be there in the morning cooking our breakfast and preparing my school lunch before I headed off for the day.

"Mamaw, these strawberries are so ripe they almost melt in my mouth. My, they are good! You know, there's nothing like strawberries and pancakes for breakfast. I wish they were ripe all year round and not just in the springtime."

"Ollie, don't eat too many of them before you head off to school," Mamaw said as she poured herself a cup of coffee and then sat down at the table across from me. "You know what strawberries will do to your stomach. Miss McCully is particular about letting you kids get up during class to go outside. And you sure wouldn't want to have an accident right there in front of all your friends, would you?"

"Mamaw, don't be silly," I said as I bit into another sweet red strawberry. "But talk about being sick, Lizzie sure has been a sight the past few weeks. What's wrong with her? She can hardly get out of bed. She says she doesn't have a fever or anything, but all she does is throw up."

"Well, Ollie," Mamaw leaned over and whispered. "Just between you and me, I think in about seven or eight months ya'll are going to have a little baby around the house."

I was shocked! I couldn't speak and I nearly choked on my strawberry! The thought of babies around the house had never entered my head. In my ten-year-old mind I had assumed that from here on it would be just Papa, Lizzie, the girls, and me. Suddenly, I felt sick.

"Mamaw, No!" I blurted out. "That's impossible! You have got to be wrong!"

"Shh! Quiet down," she whispered. "I'm not for sure, but she has all the signs of being with child. The sickness in the morning; being exhausted and puny all the time. If I were an Episcopalian rather than a Methodist, I would bet my last dollar on it!"

"But Mamaw, it's just not right for her to have a baby! Everything seems to be going so well right now."

"Ollie, what did you really expect? Lizzie just turned twenty. By that age most women have had at least one or two babies. Besides, you didn't think that she was just going to take care of the three of ya'll without putting some of her own into this family, did you? Once the idea settles with you for a while, you will be excited." She began to laugh. "Not only will that baby grow on Lizzie, but the idea will grow on you, too. Now scoot!"

Mamaw stood up and motioned toward the door. "You need to get going to school. I don't want you to be late. And as far as Lizzie is concerned, I'm only guessing that she is pregnant. Nothing is definite right now, but time will tell."

As I walked to school, I prayed as hard as I could.

Chapter 5

Mamaw, as usual, was right. Within a few months Lizzie let us know that she was pregnant and expected to have the baby around Christmas. Papa said it was going to be "the Christmas present to top all Christmas presents." I just kept my mouth shut. Lizzie started feeling better, and before long, was back to taking care of the family as she slowly grew larger and larger.

One afternoon in early December I was sitting at the kitchen table, hard at work memorizing the Preamble to the Constitution. We were going to have a history test the next day, and part of the test was to write the Preamble from memory. Miss McCully made it known that if we missed any part of it, we would have to stay after school and write it on the blackboard over and over until we got it right. I had my eyes closed reciting "... *provide for the common defense, promote the general Welfare,*" when Lizzie walked in. She began quoting "'*and secure the Blessings of Liberty, to ourselves and our Posterity.*'"

"I had to learn it, too," she said, "and I'm surprised I still know it."

I opened my eyes. As Lizzie stood there, she looked *very* pregnant. I had my doubts that she would make it to Christmas. She sat down beside me and let out a big sigh. "My shoes are killing me. I don't know if my feet are getting bigger, or these shoes are getting smaller!" She unlaced the tops of her shoes and said, "Now, that's better . . . How are the studies going?"

"They're going pretty good," I answered as I closed my book. "I think I'll do okay tomorrow."

"It's hard to believe that only two years ago I was still in school." She shook her head and laughed. "And only one year ago I got married, found myself with an instant family, and now I'm about to have a baby! Things sure can change in a hurry."

"Yes, Ma'am," I said, "they can."

Lizzie patted her tummy and remarked, "I'm getting so miserable! I can't wait until this little one is here. But at least it's not August. I think I would die if I also had to contend with the heat."

"Yes, Ma'am. I'm sure that would really make it worse."

We sat quietly for a few minutes, nobody saying a word. Lizzie obviously wanted to talk, but I just wasn't in the mood for conversation. It was the day before my birthday and I had been thinking a lot about Mama and how she used to make my birthdays so special. It was almost Christmas and this would be the third Christmas without her. It seemed harder around the holidays. I missed her so much.

There was a box of saltine crackers on the table. Lizzie picked one up and started nibbling on it. "Ollie, what do you think about this baby?"

I shrugged my shoulders. "It's okay."

We sat quietly for a few more moments. She had eaten half of the cracker and placed the uneaten half on the table. She was about to speak but hesitated, unsure about saying anything else. Then, with a hint of disappointment in her voice, she said, "Ollie, you don't seem to be excited about this baby like your sisters are. Do you want to talk about it?"

"No, Ma'am, I really don't."

She picked up the cracker and began nibbling on it again. She then stood up to leave and patted me on the hand. "That's okay," she said. "But if you change your mind, I'll be glad to listen." As she started to walk away, she paused, turned back around, and smiled. "Ollie, I wish that I could have met your mother. I know she must have been a wonderful woman, and an even more wonderful mother. I hope that I can be as good a mother to my baby as she was to you. And, Ollie, happy birthday!"

The next day, December 5, we celebrated my eleventh birthday.

Now as I look back, I wish that I had opened up to Lizzie and shared my hurts and feelings with her on that early December day. Whether it would have changed the tragic future of our family, I will never know; but it would have made us closer, and conversation between us easier. Never again did Lizzie try to get me to talk about my feelings, nor did she ever share with me her inner thoughts.

Christmas came and went without a baby, but the day after New Year's Day, 1889, Lizzie started having pains. It was late afternoon when Dr. Knox arrived. Gussie, Maude, and I were hustled over to Mamaw's house. Papa said that we would be spending the night with her, and that he would come get us in the morning.

That night as Mamaw tucked Maude and Gussie into bed, she sat down on the side of their bed and said, "Girls, you need to get a good night's sleep tonight, because tomorrow is going to be a special day. Tonight a miracle is going to happen."

That night, Stephen Decatur Parker, Jr. was born.

Early the next morning Papa woke us up. "Children, put your coats on. It's time to go home and meet the new arrival."

It had begun snowing during the night, and I remember the short walk home was quiet and calm. We tip-toed into the bedroom, and there was Lizzie in the bed, cuddling a tiny bundle all wrapped up tightly. It was cool in the room, the fireplace unable to keep the cold air from creeping in.

Papa led us up to the head of the bed to get a better look at the baby. We could hardly see him. He was all wrapped up; only his eyes and nose peeked through. Papa put his hands on my sisters' shoulders and, in a whisper, said, "Girls, what do you think about your new baby brother. His name is Stephen."

Gussie, a typical four year old, looked at the little face for a minute or two and then whined, "Papa, I'm hungry. I want some breakfast."

Six year old Maude moved over close to the bed, held out her arms, and said, "Now I have my own real live baby. Is it okay if I hold him?"

Papa kneeled down and gently replied, "No, not yet. Right now he needs to be with his mother."

Lizzie motioned for Maude to come closer and whispered softly, "Climb up here on the bed with me so you can get a closer look." She pulled the baby blanket down to let Maude see his face a little better. "Isn't he beautiful? In a few days you will be able to hold him as much as you want."

I remember feeling odd, standing there looking at Papa and Lizzie's baby. Part of me wanted to say, "Lizzie, I'm happy for you!" But another part of me wanted to shout, "No! No! Papa! This is not right! That should be my Mama there holding that baby!" But instead I just stood there and watched.

Mamaw fixed us breakfast and then headed back to her house. She said that she needed to straighten up after our stay last night, and she didn't want to be in the way while we got to know our little brother. I was left to watch after Maude and Gussie while Papa and Lizzie tended the baby.

Mid morning, Lizzie's mother and sister, Lottie, came over to visit and see the baby. With them there to look out for the girls, I was able to sneak out of the house for a while. It had stopped snowing, but the wind had picked up and it was getting colder. I thought I would freeze on the short journey down the road to Mamaw's house, but I needed to talk.

"Ollie, come on in and close that door before we both catch pneumonia," Mamaw yelled.

I came in and headed straight to the fireplace. My teeth were chattering, and I was shivering. It was a good ten minutes before I took off my coat and I still never felt warm.

"Ollie, what do you think about your little brother?" asked Mamaw. "Isn't he a darling?"

"I guess he's okay," I reluctantly answered as I warmed my hands in front of the fire. "Mamaw, I want to be happy about him being here, but I just can't. I feel guilty about it, but all I can think about is how it ought to be my Mama in there with that baby."

Mamaw had pulled her old rocking chair close to the fire and had wrapped a heavy shawl around her legs to keep warm. She stopped rocking for a moment and motioned for me to come close. "Come over here and sit down in my lap for a while," she said. "You're getting to be a big fella, but I don't think you're too big yet. In another year or two it will be a different story."

I sat down in her lap, and she wrapped the warm shawl around both of us. I was almost as tall as she was and I know I probably looked silly sitting there, but it was mighty warm and comfortable and I needed my grandmother's arms around me.

"Ollie, I wish I had all the answers and had just the right words to make everything right," she said, "but I don't. We all miss your mama, but I know you miss her the most, and that is understandable. You two were very close. But there comes a point where you have to get over the sadness and the hurt and begin dwelling on the good memories and good times you had. Keep her in your heart always, but let the sadness go and remember the happiness. Then her memory will bring you joy."

"Hold me close, Mamaw," I remember saying as I laid my head on her shoulder. "It's so cold in here."

Mamaw hugged me tightly and gently patted me on the cheek. She slowly began to rock, and I closed my eyes. For a moment I was in my Mama's lap again. As we sat there in silence, I could almost hear Mama whisper to me that she loved me more than anything else in the world.

"That sure is a sweet little baby," Mamaw said after a few minutes. "Lizzie and your father are so proud of that little Stephen. Your sister Maude couldn't be more thrilled to have her own real live doll to take care of and spoil. In a short time Gussie will be wanting to hold the baby too. Your sisters are doing so well, having a mother to love."

"It's hard to believe that a whole year has come and gone since the wedding," she continued. "And what a wedding it was! Lizzie was such a beautiful bride. And your father was so proud of her and the three of you. You the best man, so handsome and looking so tall! And Maude and Gussie were the sweetest flower girls I ever saw. They sure got the giggles walking down the aisle ahead of the bride. I have never seen the giggles get as contagious as they did that day. Even old man Hobgood started to smile. I didn't think the preacher would ever get that silly grin off his face and get those two married!

"Time just seems to fly by so fast. Stephen and Lizzie are so happy. Such a precious mother and baby. And you seem to be doing okay with your new mother, too, young man."

I shrugged my shoulders and said, "She's okay, I guess. But she is not my mother."

"No, Ollie, she is not. But she loves you so much and tries so hard. You're eleven years old, and she is only twenty, barely out of the teens herself. She had to learn fast how to handle a family. Most women start out with babies first, not half grown children, and I think she has done quite well."

"Yes, Ma'm. But I still miss Mama so much."

Chapter 6

Life settled down and the Parker family went about the business of living. Winter gave way to spring, and little Stephen was the center of our world. Lizzie was back on her feet and taking care of household duties in no time and, as she had promised, Maude was soon able to hold "her baby" as much as she wanted.

I remember Stephen was an exceptionally pretty baby. He had the bluest eyes, light brown hair with just a hint of a curl, and a chubby little face that was never without a grin. He was always happy and cried very little. I soon got used to having him around and actually began to enjoy his company.

Lizzie was a wonderful mother to Stephen. She would rock him and coo to him for hours at a time, devoting herself to his every need. She seemed the perfect mother for the perfect baby.

And Maude and Gussie were the perfect big sisters to Stephen. They loved having their own real live doll. Maude had an old doll buggy, and the two of them would stroll Stephen around the house for hours, singing him every Sunday school song they knew. As the weather warmed, the two girls moved their buggy rides outside and were soon entertaining all the neighbors with visits from "little Stephen and his mamas."

But as time passed, I started to notice a change in the way Gussie interacted with him. When Stephen was very small, she had the greatest time playing with him. As he got older and more interactive, his happy little personality drew everyone to him. Family, neighbors, and even strangers were captivated by this little tot. Gussie, who had been the baby before Stephen was born, had become accustomed to all the attention usually given to the youngest, and now that attention was directed at little Stephen. She seemed to be okay while he was a babe-in-arms, but as he got older, she obviously didn't like that she was no longer the center of attention. It all culminated one Saturday afternoon in February when Stephen was thirteen months old.

I was keeping Maude, Gussie, and Stephen while Lizzie went to the store and to visit with Mrs. Lillie Rivers down the road. It was a cold, rainy day, and we were all inside: Maude and Gussie were playing with their dolls and Stephen was having a good time playing with a toy trumpet that Papa had brought home a few weeks ago and given to Gussie.

I was lying on the floor in front of the fireplace, captivated by a book that my teacher, Miss McCully, had let me take home from school for the weekend. *The Adventures of Huckleberry Finn* by Mark Twain had been published six years earlier in 1884, and we had finally gotten a copy for our tiny school. I had already read *The Adventures of Tom Sawyer* and *The Celebrated Jumping Frog of Calaveras County* and was thrilled when Miss McCully said that we were getting *Huckleberry Finn*. As I read, I imagined that I was Huck Finn, free as a bird, with no responsibility, floating down the Mighty Mississippi with my colored friend, Jim. But the one thing about that book that disturbed me was how could any father not love his son and treat him so mean? And I remember feeling sorry for Huck for not having a Papa like mine.

As I was reading, Gussie suddenly jumped up, ran over to Stephen, yelled "That's mine!" and yanked the little trumpet out of his hand. Stephen let out a horrible scream, and in a matter of seconds, there was blood everywhere. I ran over to Stephen and saw there was blood all over his hand. I grabbed the first thing I could find, wrapped up his little hand, and yelled for Maude to run down the street and get Mamaw.

In a matter of seconds Mamaw was there. "Ollie," she panted as she tried to catch her breath. "Tell me what happened!"

"Mamaw, it happened so fast!" I frantically replied. "One moment things were fine, and the next I knew there was blood everywhere!"

She took little Stephen from my arms as I related what had happened. As I was finishing the story, I started feeling weak, like I was about to faint. I remember it sounded like I was in a cave as I said, "I wrapped up his hand . . . in a diaper . . . to try to stop . . . the bleeding."

"Ollie, you did the right thing. Let me see his hand," she said as she gently unwrapped the diaper. "Why, his little finger is gone! It must have been in one of those little holes in the horn when Gussie grabbed it. Poor thing! Maude, run to Dr. Knox's and tell him to get over here. And tell him he will need to do some stitching so he will bring what he needs. After you find him, run to Mrs. Rivers' house and get Lizzie, and to the store and get Papa." Mamaw held Stephen close, trying to get him to stop crying.

She then looked at me and asked, "Ollie, are you okay? You look awfully pale. Maybe you ought to sit down and put your head down between your legs. I don't want you fainting on me; I have my hands full right now with your little brother."

I did as she said, and in a few moments I was feeling better. The ringing in my ears stopped, and the fog I was in slowly lifted. I don't know why, but to this day, blood affects me that way and I still get faint and dizzy.

Mamaw looked around and asked, "Where is Gussie?"

"She ran outside when the hollering started," I replied as I sat up and slowly shook my head. "She knows she's in big trouble!"

"Ollie, she didn't do it on purpose. Why, she's only five years old. I know she must feel awful right now."

"I don't know about that, Mamaw," I said as I continued to feel stronger. "For the past few months Gussie's been acting strange when she's around Stephen. Sometimes she can be so mean. When he was really small, everything seemed a lot better. Gussie and Maude were always sweet to him and treated him like a little prince. When he was crying or pitching a fit, they were good about taking him from Lizzie and riding him around in the buggy. It always seemed to calm him down, and he would go right to sleep. But as he has gotten older, he has turned into such a happy, pretty baby, and everybody makes a fuss over him. I think Gussie is jealous.

"When Lizzie picks him up and plays with him, Gussie gets a mean looking frown on her face. She looks like she hates him. I don't like it, Mamaw. It's scary."

"Ollie, don't talk like that," Mamaw remarked, as she rocked Stephen, whose crying had settled down to a whimper. "A little jealousy of babies by older children is pretty normal. I remember when Maude was a baby, every time your mother would pick her up you would want to get in her lap, too."

"No, Mamaw, with Gussie it just doesn't seem right. I've seen her pinch the baby, and when he tries to sit up, Gussie will push him over if no one is looking. I even think Lizzie is worried."

"Well, we might need to keep a close eye on her. But right now we need to try and keep the baby calm until the doctor gets here. It looks like the bleeding has stopped. Poor little thing. And Ollie, you finally have a little color back in your face. I thought for a moment that I was going to have two patients to care for!"

Mamaw looked toward the door. "Where is that doctor? I wish he would hurry up and get here. I hope he's not off somewhere with an emergency. Ollie, go see if you can find out what's taking him so long."

I was feeling back to my old self and headed to the door. "There's Dr. Knox coming up the walk right now," I said as I looked out. "And Lizzie and Papa are right behind him."

"Thank the Lord!" Mamaw said. "By the way, when are you going to stop calling her Lizzie and start calling her Mother like your sisters do? She would really appreciate it, and I think you would find that you would like it, too."

"No, Mamaw, I won't."

Chapter 7

Stephen lost the little finger on his right hand, but he bounced back quickly. Within a few days he was back to his happy little self and actually started walking the next week. My theory is that his hand was hurting too much to crawl and so he just got up. As for Gussie, it's surprising how a five-year-old reacts to situations. The next day she acted as if nothing at all traumatic had happened in her little girl world, and playtime continued as usual; though, her treatment of Stephen did seem to mellow out.

In March, Papa announced that he and Lizzie had some wonderful news. Lizzie was going to have another baby, most likely in August or September. This time the news was not a shock like it had been with Stephen. Stephen was such a happy fellow, so much fun to be around. I started thinking that having babies around the house wasn't so bad after all. I found myself actually excited about the news.

As with her last pregnancy, Lizzie was sick. But with this pregnancy, her sickness was not limited to the morning hours; it was all day and all night long. She could not stand the sight or smell of anything cooking and stayed as far away from the kitchen as possible. Thankfully, Mamaw stepped in again and kept us fed and the household running. But we soon realized that Lizzie wasn't quite far enough away from the kitchen. At almost every meal, we could hear her gagging and throwing up in the bedroom, as miserable as could be. It got to where none of us wanted to eat anything and we just stared at each other over the kitchen table. Before long we were going over to Mamaw's little cottage to eat our meals in peace. Thankfully, with time, the nausea subsided and Lizzie rejoined our company.

One afternoon in April, I stopped by Mamaw's little cottage on my way home from school for a visit and some chocolate cake. Chocolate was a rare find in rural America in 1890. The bitter dark delicacy wasn't readily available. It wasn't until 1895 that Milton Hershey first sold chocolate commercially, and not until 1903 that his famous chocolate factory in Derry Township, Pennsylvania, was built, making chocolate an everyday treat throughout America. So when Mamaw was able to get her hands on some chocolate, what a treat it was!

"Mamaw, are you sure you want me to take the rest of this cake home with me?" I asked. "I think I'd rather leave it here. At home it will disappear in no time; here we'll be able to enjoy it for several days."

Mamaw frowned, shook her head, and said, "Ollie, don't tell me you're not going to share. You don't want your family to think you're selfish, do you?"

"No, Ma'am," I answered as I forced another bite of cake in my already full mouth. "But this cake is so good! And we don't have chocolate cake very often at all."

"It is a rarity," she said. "I would be glad to make chocolate cake everyday if I could. But it's hard to find chocolate. Ollie, when you leave here today, you take the rest of this cake home. I don't want to be accused of hoarding cake."

"Yes, Ma'am," I said reluctantly.

"How was school today?" Mamaw asked as she cleaned off the table and brushed the cake crumbs in her hand.

"It was fine," I answered as I finished my milk. "Today Miss McCully told us all about the Census that is being taken this year. She said that every ten years the government tries to count all the citizens. The first Census was in 1790, one hundred years ago, and the last one was ten years ago."

Mamaw thought a moment and said, "Yes, I remember the last Census. A man was going up and down our street in Meridian, writing everyone's name in a book. He said everyone needed to have his name in the book. I told him the only book I really needed my name in was the Lamb's Book of Life, and it was already in it." She laughed at her own little joke.

"Miss McCully was telling us that with this year's Census, the results will be tallied differently than ever before. She said that with the population growing the way it has, keeping track of the numbers has become almost impossible. But she said that a man by the name of Herman Hollerith from Buffalo, New York, has invented a machine that can read information off a card with holes punched in it. The machine has spring-loaded needles that pass through the holes and triggers a counter. Holes punched in various places on the cards allow you to count numerous items of information at one time. She said that a worker can feed about three hundred of the cards into the machine every hour and it will save countless hours of tedious work. They hope that the information will be more accurate than it ever has been in the past."

"Well, isn't that interesting," Mamaw's voice trailed off as she rinsed off my plate. By the way she replied, it was obvious that she hadn't understood a word I said.

Herman Hollerith went on to invent numerous tabulating and counting machines. In 1896, he formed the Tabulating Machine Company, and in 1911, his company merged with two other companies and became the Computing Tabulating Recording

(CTR) Corporation. Thirteen years later, in 1924, the company's name was changed to IBM.

"How is Lizzie doing?" Mamaw asked as she dried the plate and placed it in the cupboard.

"She's doing a lot better," I answered. "Finally getting over all that sickness. Now she's eating like a hungry little pig, like we're going to run out of food."

"There's nothing worse than sickness of pregnancy," Mamaw said as she placed the rest of the chocolate cake on a cake plate. "I remember the nauseated feeling was about as bad as actually having the baby. But then once the miracle happens and that sweet little baby is here, you forget about how difficult it is to have a baby."

"My Sunday School teacher said that if Eve hadn't eaten that apple, having a baby would be as easy as falling off a log. She said that because of her sin, God cursed women to suffer pain," I said with pride, and relief, that I was a male.

"Yes, that's what it says," Mamaw remarked. "But the blessing that God has given women to have children, the joy of bringing new life in this world, far exceeds the suffering and pain." She then laughed, pointed her finger at me, and said, "Besides, if God had given the responsibility of having babies to men, the human race would have disappeared years ago. Men can't handle pain at all, and after one baby, Adam would have said, 'No more.'"

"That new baby will be here in no time," Mamaw continued. "You know August is only four months away. I remember that when you found out that Lizzie was going to have Stephen, you were not happy at all. But I get the feeling things are different this time."

"Yes, Ma'am," I said. "Having a little brother has been a lot more fun than I expected, and I'm really looking forward to having another one around the house. Stephen is such a happy, pretty baby, and everybody just loves him so. Mrs. Matthews, the piano player at church, makes a fuss over him every Sunday morning. Last Sunday after the service, she was holding Stephen and said that she could just eat him up, he was so cute. She teased with Maude and Gussie, told them that she was going to take him home with her and keep him for good. Gussie had a great big smile on her face and told her that would be okay with her, but Maude started to cry."

"Maude is such a sensitive little girl," Mamaw interjected.

"Mrs. Matthews patted Maude on the shoulder," I continued, "and told her that she was only joking, that she was just trying to be funny. Maude stopped crying, but Gussie looked so disappointed: like she was going to start crying. She seemed upset that Stephen was coming home.

"You remember when Stephen lost his finger; I told you how jealous Gussie seemed to be about all the attention he was getting. Well, I don't think it has gotten any better. And when another baby shows up, no telling how she is going to act."

Mamaw stood up and handed me the chocolate cake and I reluctantly took it.

"Everything is going to be just fine. Now run on home and take this cake with you. And make sure you share it with everybody."

"Yes, Ma'am," I halfheartedly answered.

"And, Ollie, I agree that Gussie does tend to be a little selfish and jealous at times," she said, shooing me out the door. "But I bet when there are two babies around, she will learn to give a little."

Sadly, we would never know.

Chapter 8

One month later, on May 8, 1890, tragedy struck. Little Stephen died at fifteen months of age, ripping the heart out of our family. It started out as a simple cold—a runny nose and a fever. But after a few days the cough started. Initially it was a mild cough that didn't seem to be anything at all, but it got worse and worse. Dr. Knox said that it was whooping cough. There was an epidemic of it in Meridian which had started making its way to Lockhart.

Stephen continued to get worse. I remember the cough sounded horrible. When he would try to breathe, his little throat would spasm, and he would make the worst sound as he tried to suck air in. He would cough so hard that his face would turn red, and his eyes looked like they would explode.

Lizzie held him and rocked him all day and all night. Her mother, Charlotte, with Lottie close behind, came to help and offered to hold Stephen so that Lizzie could get some rest, but Lizzie refused to let anyone help. She was exhausted and completely worn out. She rocked him constantly, held him close, and cried.

Stephen's fever continued to get higher, and he got sicker and sicker. I remember Lizzie wiping his little face with a cool cloth and praying that God would send His cool, healing touch to her precious baby. She tried to get him to take a little soup or milk, but he couldn't keep anything down. Soon Stephen was so weak that he couldn't hold his head up.

Dr. Knox came by each day. I remember him standing with the Reverend Lewis at the crib, knowing that there was nothing medicine could offer, but hoping that the prayers of the minister would be effective.

Finally, Little Stephen was too weak to fight and he died in Lizzie's arms as she tried all she could to comfort him. Lizzie was heartbroken.

The loss of little Stephen seemed harder on me than when Mama died. As with so many times when I needed a shoulder to cry on, there was Mamaw.

The day of Stephen's funeral was dark and rainy. When we left the cemetery, Mamaw and I stopped by her cottage while the rest of the family and friends headed home.

"Ollie, come sit beside me and let's talk awhile," she said. "It's been such a sad day."

"Mamaw, I don't understand." I remember crying, "Why did he have to die? He was just a baby. He didn't hurt anybody."

"I don't understand either," Mamaw said as she put her arm around my shoulders. "But I've been around long enough to know that death is a part of life. Sometimes sickness comes and there is nothing we can do about it.

"Little Stephen was such a good baby," she continued. "He was just starting to walk. It was so much fun watching as he would take off. His little face would light up, and he would laugh and squeal when you would run after him. Nothing seemed to slow him down. Even when he lost that finger, within a day or two he was going full steam. Always so healthy and happy. But then when he got sick . . . Oh, how it hurt to see him suffer! And that cough was so horrible. Sometimes there comes a point where death is inevitable and, at that point, it is almost welcomed. The suffering is over and the pain is gone."

"But Mamaw, I prayed so hard. My Sunday school teacher said that if you pray hard enough, God will listen. He said that with prayer you can even make mountains move. Why didn't God listen to me and heal Stephen? I don't understand."

"Ollie, I don't understand either," Mamaw replied. "But don't think that God doesn't listen. He hears everything you say. In fact, do you realize that He knows what your prayers are going to be even before you pray? God knows your every thought. And he does answer your prayers. But what you will learn is that the answer is not always 'yes.' Sometimes the answer is 'no.' Just like when you ask something of your Papa, he listens, thinks about it, considers what is best, and then gives you an answer. The answer may not please you, but you do get an answer.

"It's the same with your Heavenly Father. The One who made all the heavens and the earth, Who is all-powerful and all-knowing. He doesn't grant our every wish like some genie in a bottle. In our limited minds, we truly feel that the only answer to a prayer for the healing of a little one like Stephen should be 'yes.' But God sees things differently from us. We don't understand and probably won't understand until we get to heaven and ask Him ourselves. Then things will be made known and we will understand."

"God shouldn't have let Stephen die," I argued. "It's just not right. And what about the Rolison's baby. He had the same cough as Stephen, but he got well. Everyone says that God answered their prayers and healed him. Why didn't he answer mine? And my Mama; God shouldn't have let her die either. I hate God!"

"Ollie, it is hard to understand," she said as she pulled me close. "For a young man of twelve you have had more than your share of hurt and pain; your mother and now your brother. But don't hate God for this. There is still a lot about life and death and suffering that you have to learn. In this world you will see sadness and suffering and even hate. Some of it is brought on by the choices people make and by the mistakes they make; what the Bible calls 'sin.' People suffer the consequences of their bad choices.

"At other times there is no explanation; bad things just happen. But, Ollie, there is a lot of good in this world, a lot of joy and love. We praise God and thank Him for all the good we have. But when bad occurs, you can't turn your back on Him. That just isn't right. In all things, good and bad, even when you don't deserve it or even understand it, you have to praise Him and trust Him. If you do, you will find that He will help you get through it. He will help you carry the burden, make it a little lighter. And why Mrs. Rolison's baby was healed and Stephen was not, I don't know. That is one of the many questions we will ask Jesus when we get to heaven."

I sat quietly for a few moments, thinking about how horrible the day had been. "Mamaw," I said, "it sure was a mess at the cemetery."

"Yes it was. Such a difficult and sad day. Funerals are bad enough, but this rain made it so miserable. Everyone got soaked to the bone. I'm so glad that your parents decided not to take Maude and Gussie to the cemetery. Lizzie's mother and Lottie were so kind to keep them during the service. It would have been too much for them. And seeing your mother and father, heartbroken, dripping wet was almost more than I could bear. But it is over now. Everyone should be at the house by now, trying to get dry."

"Mamaw, I'm glad we stopped at your house. I don't feel like going home right now."

"I felt you and I needed a little time together. You know, it's a strange thing when someone dies," she mused. "You want to be alone, but you also want people to be with you and let you know they care. Lizzie has done well. She is having such a hard time with losing little Stephen but has welcomed family and visitors so graciously. And yet, she knows that there are times when she has to be alone with your father to mourn.

"Little Stephen's death has just broken her heart. Twenty-two years old and losing her little baby. And another baby on the way in only three months. Try to understand that she will not be herself during this time. Her thoughts will seem to be far away, and she may not give you and your sisters the attention that you are used to. You are old enough to understand, but your sisters will find it hard. It's up to us and your father to try to make their home as happy as we can for them."

Mamaw paused for a few moments then continued. "Ollie, I guess it's about time to head over to the house and join the family and friends."

"No, Mamaw, not yet," I said as I pulled close to her. "Let's don't go yet. Let's sit here a while longer." I was not ready to leave the quiet of Mamaw's home and face the activity at mine.

Mamaw continued to rock and said, "We can wait a little longer; we're not in any big hurry. But in a little while we do need to go and thank our friends and family. Everyone has been so good to us through all this. You really learn the value of family, friends, and church during times like this. And one thing that people *do* know how to do when there is a death is cook," she said with a smile. "So much food! You could feed a small army. And the ladies of the church have been so good at taking turns at the house, welcoming visitors, preparing meals, and watching after your sisters. What would we do if it weren't for them?"

Mamaw frowned and shook her head. "And yet at times I wonder about people. The things they say to try to comfort people when they hurt. At the wake yesterday, I heard Mrs. Hodges say to your mother, 'Isn't it wonderful that you have another baby on the way who will take little Stephen's place? Before long your love will be so wrapped up in the new one that you won't even remember losing him.' I couldn't believe she said that! In trying to comfort, some people just stab you in the heart and don't even know it. I could just see the hurt in your mother's eyes. Thank goodness Charlotte was sitting beside Lizzie. She stood up and kindly walked Mrs. Hodges to the other side of the room. You don't replace babies like you do a cup that drops and breaks. Yes, she will have a baby to put her love into, but the idea of erasing the memory of little Stephen . . . You don't ever want to forget your baby. Sad to say it, but for your sisters, that's what will happen. At age eight and five, they will forget easily. When the new baby comes along, their thoughts of Stephen will fade away."

Mamaw was quiet for a moment. Then she smiled and said, "Ollie, did you notice at the cemetery that your father left a space between your mother and little Stephen?"

"No, Mamaw, I didn't."

"He plans to be buried there beside her. I know you have been concerned that she would be forgotten. But as you can see, your father hasn't forgotten her, and he never will. He still loves her very much."

I remember resting my head on Mamaw's shoulder and softly crying as I thought of my mother and of little Stephen.

After a few minutes, Mamaw stood up and kissed me on the forehead. "It's time to go home." She looked at my face. "My, my, you are looking so much like your mother! When I look into your eyes, it's like seeing her look back at me."

"Yes, Ma'am. That's what Papa says too."

Chapter 9

In spite of Stephen's death, that summer was one of best times of my life. There is nothing better than being twelve years old in Mississippi, where the days are long and the summers are hot. I would get up at daybreak, head over to Mamaw's house where I would meet Lizzie's brothers, Junius and James, for a breakfast of bacon, eggs, and pancakes, before heading off for a day of swimming, fishing, or exploring the deep woods of central Mississippi.

One of our favorite spots was where Lost Horse Creek emptied into Ponta Creek, about three miles from the house. We would follow the railroad track north and then cut through the woods on a trail that we *knew* Indians had made. There was an old Indian mound on the west bank of Ponta Creek and we would spend hours looking for arrowheads and pieces of broken pottery. There was an ancient oak standing in the fork of the two creeks. We rigged up an old rope swing on one of its lower branches and would compete to see who could land the farthest in the warm, muddy water.

Some days Mamaw would pack us up a supper and a few biscuits for breakfast and we would spend the night looking at the stars as we slept on top of the old Indian mound. Those were good times, when you are old enough to have a little freedom, but still too young to have much responsibility. The freedom of that summer and the ability to spend hours and days away from the house helped me to cope with and sometimes forget about our family's loss.

Back at the house Lizzie was learning to cope with little Stephen's death. She spent most of that summer in bed, resting. Dr. Knox felt that the strain of losing Stephen was too much for her, and for the sake of her unborn child, she needed bed rest. She didn't lack for entertainment, though. Maude and Gussie were in, on, and around her bed throughout the day playing dolls and dress up. Their presence did more than anything else to lift her spirits and prevent her from going crazy with grief. Lizzie's mother and sister, Lottie, came by almost every afternoon, and neighbors dropped by several times a week to visit. And Mamaw, as always, stepped right in and carried on with the household duties.

In August 1890, Timothy Woods Parker was born. Having remembered how much fun little Stephen had been as a baby, I was excited about the new arrival. But what a difference! Timothy cried constantly. He was miserable, and he made us miserable. He cried when he ate and he cried when he didn't eat; he cried when he was picked up and he cried when he was put down. Nothing seemed to please him. Lizzie did her best but she couldn't make him happy. Maude and Gussie tried the buggy routine that worked so well with Stephen, but they eventually gave up.

Timothy was a sick baby. He always seemed to have a fever and runny nose. He was thin and bony, and looked like he would just shrivel up and blow away. Dr. Knox came to visit him frequently, but could not find anything wrong. He said what the baby needed was nourishment, and that Lizzie needed to feed him more frequently. She fed him constantly; at least that was the way it looked to me. When he ate, he would act hungry, almost fighting for her breast. But as soon as he started to suckle he would tighten his stomach, arch his back, and throw up everything he had just eaten.

The family worried about little Timothy. But Maude and Gussie got tired of him; they didn't want anything to do with him. When he would start his crying, eight-year-old Maude would let out a frustrating sigh, get up, and leave the room. Five-year-old Gussie would stomp over to his crib and yell at him to be quiet. At times she would grab the railing on the crib and shake it as hard as she could. I worried what might happen if she was alone with him.

Chapter 10

One afternoon in November, I made my usual stop at Mamaw's house on my way home from school.

"How was school today?" Mamaw asked as she handed me a glass of milk and a bowl filled with the best blackberry cobbler in all of Lauderdale County.

"It was fine," I answered as I took a healthy bite. "But Miss McCully told us today that she will no longer be teaching after Christmas. She's getting married."

"I heard she was getting married. Marrying Clelia Hill's boy is what I heard. Why is she not going to teach any more? Are they moving away after the wedding?"

"No, Ma'am," I answered. "She said that the county won't let her teach after she gets married. Something about a rule the school board had passed a few years back. She'll still be here and would like to keep on teaching but can't."

"That makes no sense," she said as she shook her head. "It's hard enough to find teachers who are willing to come to our little town, and when one does stupid rules run them off. She's one of the best teachers this place has had in a long time. Trained in Birmingham I heard, smart as a whip, and so pleasant. It's going to be hard to replace her. And who's going to move here in the middle of the winter?

"One thing that really burns me up," she fumed, "is that if she were a male teacher and getting married, there would not be a problem at all. It's just not right the way women are treated in this country. Ollie, can you believe that women don't even have the right to vote?"

"Yes, Ma'am," I answered with a full mouth. "We learned that in government class."

"And what makes it even harder to believe," she continued, "is that they passed a law a few years ago that lets *colored* people vote! Who would have ever believed it! Letting them have more rights than us women. But I hear that up North women are getting together and marching, demanding that we have the right to vote. I read in the newspaper a month or two ago that an organization was formed."

"Yes, Ma'am. It's The National American Woman Suffrage Association," I chirped in. Miss McCully was smarter than a lot of people realized. She had been planting seeds of women's rights in our minds. "We learned about that in school, too. Susan B. Anthony is their president."

"My, my, you are a smart one!" Mamaw declared. "I sure hope they can get something done in Washington."

"I can't wait for Thanksgiving," I said, changing the subject. "Mamaw, this cobbler is so good! I hope you still have enough blackberries to make another one for Thursday."

"I sure do!" answered Mamaw. "Remember we picked about two gallons of them in July and I still have enough put up to make another three or four cobblers."

"Oh, I remember!" I said shaking my head as I thought back on that hot July morning. "I don't think I have ever sweated that much in my life! And the chiggers! I don't know why they're always around blackberry bushes, but I was covered with itchy whelps for two weeks. Thank goodness for Calamine Lotion!"

"The itching *was* bad, but those blackberries sure are worth it!" Mamaw said. "And by the way, men and women don't sweat. *Horses* sweat, men perspire, and women glow!" She laughed at her own little joke.

"What else are we having for Thanksgiving?" I asked as I downed another bite of cobbler.

"Lizzie's cooking a turkey and a ham, and Charlotte's bringing a green bean casserole, creamed corn, and sweet potatoes. I'm in charge of the desserts. In addition to the cobbler, there will be plenty of apple pie, pumpkin pie, and chocolate cake! You and Junius and James won't be disappointed. And talking about eating, how is little Timothy doing?"

"Mamaw, I worry about him," I answered as I started on my second helping of cobbler. "He cries all the time."

"Too bad you can't remember when you were a baby," she laughed. "Your brother doesn't hold a candle to the hollering you could do. Your first summer was one of the hottest I ever remembered. And it was so hot and humid that the bed sheets would literally stick to you at night. No breeze at all. You were about eight months old that August, and I can still remember how you would wail at the top of your lungs when your mama would try to put you down. It was just too hot to even think about sleep! A lot of nights your father would take you outside and walk you up and down the road to try to catch any breeze he could to cool you off and get you to hush. I'm sure the neighbors really appreciated the serenade."

"I'm trying to be serious, Mamaw," I said as I frowned. "Timothy is just not right. He is not a healthy baby."

"I'm sorry, Ollie. I was just remembering when you were little. You are right about little Timothy. He worries me, too. Nothing seems to make him happy. I've never seen a baby that is so hard to please. It's wearing poor Lizzie down. I don't think she gets any rest at all."

"No, she doesn't." I paused for a moment and continued. "I'm worried about Gussie, too. I think she is going to hurt Timothy. The way she acts when he cries, you can see hate in her eyes. Yesterday when he was particularly fussy and loud, which is most of the time, she yelled at him to stop. She picked up a pillow and headed to the crib. She pushed it down on his face and would have held it there till he stopped breathing if Papa had not grabbed her. Papa whipped her really good and told her to never do that again, but it didn't seem to faze her at all. I think she would do it again if she had the chance."

"Ollie, for heaven's sake, Gussie is only five years old, and you're making her out to be some devil child. I agree that she is a very high-strung little girl, but she's not a bad person. She just doesn't realize the consequences of what she is doing. Children that age don't have the maturity to see beyond the next minute. And with Timothy's constant crying, I sometimes get extremely frustrated myself."

"Yes, Ma'am, but I don't think you would try to smother him to death," I retorted.

"I'll talk to your father. We do need to keep a close eye on her and Timothy. But for now, young man, finish up your cobbler and scoot! Let me get back to my cooking. Thanksgiving is almost here and I know you want me to have everything ready."

"Yes, Ma'am, I can't wait!"

Chapter 11

In February 1891, when Timothy was almost five months old, something miraculous happened. Thanks to the advice of one of our neighbors, he was introduced to goat's milk. And what a difference that made!

Most afternoons after school, and after a slice of Mamaw's pie, I would head down to the store to help Papa with whatever needed to be done—sweeping, stocking, loading goods into wagons. On this cold, rainy February afternoon, while I stacked bags of sugar on a shelf, Papa and several men were standing around the old pot-belly stove warming their hands, and their backsides. It was not uncommon on rainy days, when nothing much could be done around the farms, for men to gather at the store and catch up on the local news and find out what was going on in the world.

During a lull in the conversation, Mr. Rivers looked over at me and asked, "Ollie, how is your little brother doing? Is he still having problems eating?"

"Yes, sir," I answered as I continued to stock the shelf. "He's not doing very well. All he does is throw up and cry."

"He's not gaining weight like he should," Papa interjected. "He's skinny as a rail and is sick all the time. We're really worried about him."

"That's too bad," Mr. Rivers replied. "What does Dr. Knox recommend?"

"He told Lizzie to feed him more often," Papa answered, "that he needed more nourishment; but it's not working."

"You might want to try goat's milk for that baby," Mr. Rivers remarked. "You know, a few years back my sister's baby had the same problem. They started giving him goat's milk and it really helped settle his stomach."

"Well it's worth a try," Papa said. "I think I would try anything at this point to help that poor little fellow. Does anyone know where I can find a goat?"

Several days later, Papa was able to find and purchase an old nanny goat, and I was given the task of milking her. What an experience that was! I had been milking cows since I could walk and found it pretty easy and straightforward, but milking a goat was a real battle! That old goat was mean, and we never got along at all. When I would open up the pen and walk in to do the milking, she would put her head down and run full steam straight at me. The first few encounters I found myself flat on my back, but I soon learned to grab her by the ears with both hands and back her up in a corner. But there was no way to milk her when both hands were needed just to keep her still. I enlisted the help of eight year old Maude to actually do the milking while I held on to the goat, and before long we mastered the art of goat milking.

Goat's milk was a gift from heaven; a miracle cure. Up until this point, Lizzie had been feeding him breast milk exclusively. When she introduced Timothy to the goat's milk, he took to it like a bear to honey. Within a week's time, we saw a total transformation occur in that little fellow. He changed from a howling, miserable, sickly child to one that was unbelievably happy and healthy. Lizzie then started giving him solid food: mashed up rice, potatoes, carrots, and peas. He started gaining weight, and actually began to smile and laugh.

To say the least, we were completely dumbfounded, and very grateful. Mamaw said that her prayers had finally been answered and her sanity restored. And with this heaven-sent change in our little brother there was no more screaming and hollering. Maude and I continued to wrestle the wonder elixir from that old goat with no complaint at all!

Looking back, it's obvious that Timothy was allergic to Lizzie's milk. In that day nothing was really known about food allergies. We all knew that if we ate certain things it would make us sick, give us a stomach ache, or make us throw up, and we learned to stay away from those foods. But the idea of being allergic to your own mother's milk was not something we could comprehend. But, we didn't complain one bit. Our home became a happy place again.

With Timothy's new-found health, Maude and Gussie developed a new-found interest in their little brother. They began to play with him. The buggy rides through the house were reminiscent of a year before with little Stephen. Papa bought a small wagon just the right size to hitch up that old goat, and when the weather got a little warmer, the girls would pile in the wagon and take Timothy riding through the neighborhood. Also, to my relief (and I'm sure everyone else's), there was no fear of leaving Gussie alone with the baby.

Life settled down again for the Parker family. Winter gave way to spring, and spring to summer. Unlike last summer, this summer I spent more time around the house. Timothy was there, healthy and happy, and the sadness of last summer when Stephen's had just died was a distant memory. Junius, James, and I did have a great summer swimming, fishing, and just lazing around, but I also enjoyed spending time at home.

Early one Saturday morning in late August 1891, Papa loaded us up in the wagon for one of our usual trips to Meridian. But instead of coming home Saturday night like we usually did, he said we were going to spend a couple of days in Meridian and stay with his brother and his family. The county fair was in town, and he wanted us to enjoy the festivities. Papa made arrangements with a neighbor to feed the chickens and look after the cows and the goat. I had never been to a county fair, but Junius and James had been to one in Tennessee before they had moved and had told me that it was the most fun they had ever had.

We arrived at Uncle John's house around noon, and after the usual greetings and hugs, we all headed down to the fairgrounds. Lizzie was holding the girls by the hand and Mamaw was carrying Timothy. Papa and I were following along behind, taking our time, but I was about to bust, wanting to get there as quickly as I could.

"Maude and Gussie," Mamaw said as she waddled along with Timothy in her arms, "don't let go of your mother's hand when we are at the fair. There are always gypsies around, and before you can bat an eye, they will grab you, stuff you in a sack, and carry you off and sell you to a Chinese slave ship, and we won't ever see you again."

I'd never seen two little girls hold so tightly to their mother's hand! You couldn't have pried them away from Lizzie.

"Maude, I don't think you need to worry," Papa said. "Those gypsies won't steal you; only Gussie, because she's the youngest."

Gussie's eyes got big. She stopped in her tracks and started pulling on Lizzie's hand, ready to head home.

Lizzie shook her head and frowned at Papa and Mamaw. "Stephen, don't tease the girls. There is no sense in getting them all upset. We want them to enjoy the fair and not worry that something is going to happen to them."

Papa laughed and said, "Lizzie, I'm only joking. Girls, nothing is going to happen to either one of you. Let's go have some fun!"

Interestingly, gypsies do play a significant role in the history of Meridian. In 1915, "the Queen of the Gypsies," Kelly Mitchell, died at age forty-seven of childbirth complications while her tribe was encamped near Meridian; she was buried in Rose Hill Cemetery. Her body lay in state for fifteen days at Horace Smith's Undertaking Company while five thousand members of her clan gathered from all over the United States to pay their respects. I was thirty-eight years old at the time, visiting family in Meridian, and I remember what an unbelievable disruption that funeral caused the city. Rose Hill Cemetery became a "southern burial ground" for gypsies and over the years there have been numerous tribe members buried there, but none with the pomp and circumstance of the queen. In 1942, Kelly's husband, Emil, "the King of the Gypsies," was buried next to his wife.

The fair was more than I could have imagined. There were painted wagons and tents lined up along the midway with men standing at the entrance sporting tattoos and gaudy coats, inviting "one and all" to come in and see "pygmies from Africa, sheep with two heads, a man with only one eye in the middle of his head, and a woman with the body of a snake." For a nickel you could go in and see exotic dancers who had danced before the Maharaja in India.

I remember stopping in front of the tent and asking, "Papa, can we go in and see the dancers. They came all the way from India."

"No, son," Papa answered, "it is not suitable for good Christians to see such things as that." But as we passed by, I noticed Papa straining his neck to get a glimpse through the curtains.

In the exhibit hall there were contests to see who had the best of almost anything you could think of: jellies, pies, corn, peas, quilts, tomatoes, and more. Mamaw looked at one of the pies and remarked that she would be embarrassed if that was the best she could do. In the barn there were calves and lambs that were so cleaned and scrubbed that they almost shined; and there were horses being groomed, ready to compete for "best of the fair."

There was food everywhere. The Ladies' Clubs in Meridian had prepared all types of food to raise money for their different charities, and their bountiful booths were set up under shade trees and were overflowing with fresh cooked vegetables, fried chicken, and homemade pies and cakes, all of which we thoroughly enjoyed.

As we downed all these wonderful goodies, Mamaw shook her head and said, "I'm a little concerned about eating this food. It looks okay, but no telling what kind of kitchen this food came from. I'm afraid we might come down with some horrible disease."

Between bites Papa said, "Mother, this food is just fine. I don't think there is anything at all to worry about. It's not nearly as good as yours, but let's enjoy it." Before long Mamaw was joining us and sampling tasty treats from almost every booth at the fair.

That day I had my first taste of taffy. What a treat! There is nothing like good sticky saltwater taffy, sticking to your teeth and melting in your mouth! I made myself sick, stuffing three and four pieces in my mouth at a time.

I also had my first glass of Coca-Cola. Coca-Cola had been formulated five years before in Atlanta and was rapidly becoming a popular drink throughout the country. A man was mixing a foamy water he called "soda water" with a thick brown syrup, making an odd drink that bubbled. I remember thinking what a strange, almost addictive, tasty drink. It had a fizzy bite to it and gave you gas. Mamaw got so upset with me for taking big swallows and then letting out the loudest, deepest belches we had ever heard. Maude, Gussie, and little Timothy thought my new-found talent was hilarious and kept asking me to do it again and again. Maude said that I sounded like an old bullfrog. Mamaw thought it was terrible and said that civilized people don't act like that. I should know better than to teach my siblings such dreadful habits. (Three years later, in 1894, at Joseph Biedenharn's candy store in Vicksburg, Mississippi, Coca-Cola would be bottled for the first time, opening it to a huge market, allowing me to have my favorite drink anytime and anywhere I wanted.)

That night I witnessed my first fireworks display. It was like seeing thousands of shooting stars at one instant in all the colors of the rainbow. I remember thinking that it was the most unbelievable, most impressive thing I had ever seen. Maude and Gussie stood with their mouths open during the entire show. Mamaw said this must be how the sky will look when Jesus comes back to earth to take us home to heaven.

The fair ended that night, and I couldn't wait to get back to Little Lockhart to tell James and Junius all about it. But the next day was Sunday, and my trip home would have to wait until after church.

Mamaw was excited about attending her former church, South Side Methodist, and was able to catch up on all the happenings and gossip that she had missed over the past few years while away from Meridian. (In 1915, South Side Methodist's name was changed to Hawkins Memorial.) This sacred place of worship is where, a few years ago, Papa and his brothers and sisters were reared in the faith and were taught the wonders of heaven and the fires of hell. And in only a few years, this is where the Parker family, sad and broken, would return, leaving the community and cemetery of Lockhart behind.

My return to Lockhart was further delayed by Sunday dinner. Mamaw, Lizzie, and Uncle John's wife, Florence, prepared a small Southern feast: fried chicken, sugar cured ham, butter beans, snap peas, sweet corn, and the best homemade biscuits in the whole state of Mississippi. Mamaw's sweet potato pie was the crowning glory.

After dinner, Papa, Uncle John, and I retreated to the porch with little Timothy for a visit and fresh air while the ladies did the dishes. Unlike Papa, who was rather quiet and reserved, Uncle John was a talker. He always had a story and was always making us laugh with some of his tales. He knew everyone in Meridian and everything about them, the good and the not so good. (Uncle John would later become mayor of Meridian.)

As soon as we sat down, Uncle John started one of his discourses—this one on the word "dinner."

"Fellas," he began, "let me educate you on the proper use of the word 'dinner.' You may think that anytime you sit down and eat a meal, except for breakfast of course, you can call it 'dinner.' But I'm here to tell you that this is wrong. Here's the way it really is." He scooted up on the edge of his seat and continued, talking with his hands almost as much as with his voice. "The noon meal on Sunday is always 'dinner' no matter how much food is prepared. Every other day of the week the noon meal is 'lunch,' unless it is an unusually large meal for some special occasion, and then you can call it 'dinner' if you want to. The night meal is 'supper.' 'Dinner' can be interchanged with 'supper,' but not very often, mainly when company has been invited to the meal. As we are well aware, Sunday dinner is always the best laid out meal of the week, and no matter where the meal is being prepared, the eldest of the women folk is always in charge, and the lady of the house is always second in command." He leaned forward and looked around as if checking to make sure no one else was listening. "I need to warn you. I have learned from experience that the presence of one of the men folk in the kitchen on Sunday is grounds for expulsion from the dinner table."

Papa and I laughed and nodded in agreement with Uncle John's little speech.

After the dishes were washed and dried, we packed up the wagon and headed back to Little Lockhart, leaving the big city and the thrill of the fair far behind.

Later that evening before dark, I headed over to Junius and James's house to tell them all about my day at the fair. I knew they would be so excited to hear my story. But as excited as I was to tell them my story, they seemed more interested in telling me theirs.

Having been to a fair in Tennessee, which was "larger and better than the one in Meridian," Junius and James constantly interrupted me, telling me about the wonders of *their* fair. Before long I just listened to them and didn't open my mouth.

Over the years I have often thought about that so-called conversation with the Bludworth boys. As I think back, I realize it made me a better listener. When people tell you a story, they are interested in *you* listening to *them,* rather than you playing "one upsmanship."

Chapter 12

The following week, August 31, 1891, Timothy had his first birthday. Maude, the nine year old self-proclaimed "little mama" to Timothy, helped Mamaw bake two chocolate cakes for the occasion—one small "baby cake" for Timothy to have all his own and another one for the rest of us. Little Timothy didn't understand all the excitement, but he thoroughly enjoyed his little cake. We laughed as we watched him use both hands to stuff cake in his mouth, but it looked like more of the cake ended up in his hair and ears.

The next day Timothy developed a mild case of diarrhea: Mamaw said he had eaten too much chocolate cake and it had given him the "runs." At first we weren't concerned, but over the next few days, he continued to have loose stools and he seemed more fussy than normal. After about a week he began running a low fever and he didn't want to eat. The diarrhea suddenly got more frequent, and Lizzie seemed to be changing diapers almost hourly.

Dr. Knox came to the house to check him out. He felt Timothy's stomach and looked down his throat. He said that his stomach was bloated and tender and his liver felt enlarged. Dr. Knox thought for a minute and then said, "It looks like typhoid fever. We haven't had a case of it around here in years, but I hear there's been an outbreak of it in Meridian. It started shortly after the fair left town, and a lot of people have been coming down with it.

Babies are particularly susceptible and many of them are having a pretty rough time with it."

Papa was sitting in a chair as he listened to Dr. Knox. He leaned forward and put his face in his hands and quietly said, "Our family was at the fair two weeks ago, the last day it was in town."

Dr. Knox nodded his head, feeling proud of his astute observation and diagnosis, and declared, "Well, with that information, there's not much doubt in my mind that that's what he has."

Typhoid fever is caused by an intestinal parasite similar to one that causes Salmonella, but worse. Like Salmonella, typhoid fever is most commonly seen in crowded areas with poor sanitation and contaminated water. A big gathering like the fair, where sanitation is very suspect, is a prime opportunity for this little demon to raise its ugly head. The disease is usually a self-limiting problem in adults and older children, but in infants the mortality can be fairly high. Today in the United States, typhoid fever is very uncommon; good sanitation has made it a rarity and, thankfully, with antibiotic treatment and hydration, death is unusual. But, in the 1890's, the disease was quite common. There was no treatment; no antibiotics or intravenous fluids; only fluids and loving care.

Timothy's diarrhea became much worse and his fever increased. Lizzie tried to get him to drink liquids, but he wouldn't even try. He continued to get weaker, and soon he was too weak to hold his head up. I remember Lizzie holding him close, rocking slowly and crying. It was so reminiscent of two years before when we had watched Stephen die. Dr. Knox came by every day, but said there was nothing he could do. The Reverend Lewis also came. I can still see him standing beside Lizzie and the baby, with his hand on Papa's shoulder, praying for God's divine intervention. Soon Timothy began to have convulsions, and on September 15, 1891, two weeks after his first birthday, he died.

Timothy was buried next to little Stephen in the Lockhart Cemetery. Unlike when Stephen was buried, this day was hot, unusually so for this time of year. The sun was bright and there was not a cloud in the sky. The leaves of the sweet gum trees were just starting to change to a dark rusty red. It just didn't seem right to bury someone on such a beautiful day. Maude and Gussie attended this time, holding Mamaw's hands throughout the service.

Nine year old Maude was heartbroken. I remember her soft little sobs as the minister spoke of heaven and hope. Six year old Gussie complained the entire time about how hot it was and that she was starting to sweat. She wanted to go inside and get a glass of water. Lizzie's mother, Charlotte, quietly took Gussie by the hand and walked her over to the church.

The funeral was well-attended, more so than when Stephen had died. Our family had lost, not one, but two babies in the span of two years, and the empathy and sympathy had really touched our community. Several of Mamaw's friends from Hawkins Memorial Church in Meridian made the hot, two and a half hour buggy ride to attend. Having visited with Mamaw only three weeks before Timothy's death, her friends felt a renewed bond with her and wanted to show their support.

And at the house, an overwhelming expression of sympathy was displayed on the dining room table. Dishes of food were everywhere; more food than we could possibly eat. So much food that Papa invited everyone to stay and help us eat it. (In those days there was no refrigerator to delay spoilage, just small ice boxes big enough to hold milk and butter.)

Food and Death. Food is such a time-honored way of show-ing that you care when someone dies. I've often wondered why: maybe it's saying, "I can't take away your sorrow, but I can help make your life a little easier while you grieve."

Everything seemed so similar and reminiscent of when Stephen died and was buried, except for Lizzie. She cried and cried while Timothy was sick and was continually praying that he would get well. But when he died, she changed. The day after he died, she did not come out of her bedroom and did not eat. She allowed no one in her room except Papa and her mother, Char-lotte. But on the day of the funeral she emerged a different per-son. There seemed to be no more sorrow, no more tears, at least none that we could see. She went about greeting the visitors and family with a smile and an expression that would make you won-der if this was a wedding rather than a funeral.

Her changed demeanor reminded me of the story of David in the Bible, when the son that Bathsheba bore him got sick and died. While the baby was ill, David fasted and prayed continuously. But when news came to him that the baby had died, he got up, washed himself, put on new clothes, and asked for something to eat. When his servants inquired about the sudden change in atti-tude after the child's death, David said that while the baby was alive, he had hoped that God would show mercy and heal him, but now that he was dead, there was no need to fast. "It won't bring him back to life," he said. "I shall go to him, but he shall not re-turn to me." (II Samuel 12:23) I wished that this had been the case with Lizzie.

Chapter 13

The funeral was on Sunday, and on Monday I went to school as usual. After school, I stopped by Mamaw's house for some of her sweet potato pie and milk. But more than her pie, I needed her love and words of wisdom.

"How are you doing today?" Mamaw asked as I opened the screen door and walked in.

"Fine, I guess," I replied and shrugged my shoulders. "But it was hard to concentrate after yesterday."

"I know," she said as she gave me a hug. "I've had a hard time thinking about anything else myself. We will miss little Timothy, won't we?"

She turned back to the kitchen counter and began whipping up some cream and sugar, the perfect topping for "sweet 'tater pie," as my grandfather used to call it. After a moment she paused, looked out the kitchen window, and sighed, "Didn't you think that Reverend Lewis gave such a touching and wonderful message? That verse he quoted from Revelation 21 is so comforting; it's one of my favorite scriptures in the whole Bible. 'And God shall wipe away all tears from their eyes; and there shall be no more death, neither sorrow, nor crying, neither shall there be any more pain: for the former things are passed away.' That gives me so much comfort, knowing that when we get to heaven there will be no sadness and none of the heartbreak that this world brings."

"Mamaw," I said, almost crying, "you were right about eating at the fair; we shouldn't have eaten anything there. Dr. Knox thinks that is why Timothy got sick. If we had listened to you, he would probably be just fine. I feel so guilty: I was the one who wanted so badly to go to the fair. It's my fault."

"Ollie! Don't say such a thing!" Mamaw exclaimed. She stopped what she was doing, walked over, and wrapped her arms around me. "You had nothing to do with his getting sick. We all wanted to go and we all enjoyed the food."

Mamaw patted me on the back, and then walked back over to the counter and started whipping the cream again. "If anyone is at fault," she said with her back to me, "it would be me. Letting a little baby eat food from no telling where." She straightened up her back and continued. "But there is no blame to give. Things like this happen and there is no one responsible."

In my thirteen-year old mind, I truly believed that I was responsible for Timothy's death. I hurt so badly and felt so guilty. I learned later that my response was not at all uncommon. In family tragedies, such as death, divorce, or disharmony, children will sometimes see themselves as the cause or the center of the conflict. They will come up with all kinds of reasons that it happened because of something they did or didn't do. It took me years to come to the realization that I was not at fault for any of my brothers' and sisters' deaths. I've learned that it's very important that families openly discuss death and tragedy, help children understand what happened, and make sure that they don't harbor any ideas that they are to blame.

"Mamaw, I just don't understand," I said as I took a bite of pie. "Why does God allow things like this to happen? It makes no sense to me. If He loves us the way the Bible says, why doesn't He stop suffering and death?"

"Ollie, you have asked one of the biggest questions that mankind has ever asked, and I don't think anyone has ever come up with an answer that satisfies everyone." Mamaw was rinsing off some dishes, but stopped, dried her hands, and came over and sat down beside me. "I've often pondered that question. I've searched the scriptures, but still I haven't come up with a completely satisfactory answer. And when you are in the middle of grief, it's even harder to understand and make sense. But let me tell you the way I see it."

Mamaw took a deep breath and began. "First off, God is in control and He knows what He is doing. That is first and foremost. If for no other reason, that's good enough for me. But I think that when He formed this world, He decided to put some bumps in the road. He didn't want to give us everything on a silver platter. He made it so that every day is not sunny, every season is not spring, every moment is not happy. But He did give us plenty of good days and happy days that we can truly enjoy. If every day was spring, before long a beautiful spring day would mean nothing. If every person was as beautiful as your mother was, before long everyone would look plain. If everything was perfect and all things turned out perfectly, this earth would soon be a pretty boring place. God knew what He was doing.

"Secondly," she continued, "in the scriptures it says that 'All things work together for the good of those who love and obey the Lord.' Notice it doesn't say 'All things that happen *are* good for those who love and obey the Lord.' Bad things happen to good people. God made it to where we have to work to survive. If we don't work, we will soon starve. But then He made it to where even if we work, if we do everything we can, things may happen to where we starve anyway. And likewise, if we try to do everything right, bad things may still happen to us. We have to come to grips with the fact that even if we follow God's plan and do everything we can to live a good Christian life, life may not turn out the way we want it. And when bad things happen, we have two choices. We can either blame God and become bitter toward Him, or we can accept what has happened, continue to trust God, and hope for good to come out of our hardships. Which choice do you think will work the best?

"Thirdly, why do we see evil thrive, and so often good destroyed? That is a hard one. The Bible also says that 'It rains on the just as well as the unjust.' In our minds good should be rewarded and evil punished . . . *NOW*. We are so impatient! I truly believe that evil will be punished and good rewarded, but not necessarily in the timeframe that we want. God is in control, and 'judgment belongs to the Lord.'

"And Ollie, God truly does love us. Even though He made this world with bumps in the road and raging rivers to cross, He still loves us and wants the best for us. In fact, He loved us so much that He sent his Son, Jesus, to die for us. No matter what happens, if we trust in Jesus, He will help us come through any hardship a better person."

"Yes, Ma'am," I responded, "but it hurts so bad. And it's hard to find happiness in what has happened."

"Ollie, I didn't say we are to be happy when bad things happen," she corrected me. "I said that we should look to God for comfort, and trust that in all things He will bring about good. And Ollie, it does hurt. Things like Timothy's and Stephen's death will rip your heart out, and grieving and hurting is a normal response. You have to let yourself grieve. But always in the back of your mind know that God is there. He will see you through it."

What profound wisdom from a little country lady. Even today I marvel at the words she spoke that day.

"Mamaw, I don't understand Lizzie," I said as I took another bite of pie and whipped cream. "Yesterday at the funeral she just didn't seem to be normal. She seemed unusually happy and cheerful: I don't think she shed a single tear all day. And this morning, while she was fixing breakfast, she was humming and singing like it was Christmas. She was talking about all the people who came by yesterday and how she enjoyed visiting with them. She went on about how our house is so well laid out to entertain guests; that she really should invite people over more often, and not just when there is a funeral. Papa just sat there and didn't say a word, but he looked awfully concerned at what she was saying. When Stephen died, and even when Timothy was sick, she was so upset; but now . . . I just don't know."

A worried look came over Mamaw's face. She stood up and took my empty plate and glass to the sink. After a moment she said, "Ollie, Lizzie has been through so much. Such a young mother to have lost two little babies. Over the past two weeks she has shed more tears than you can count, and I think that the sadness has gotten the best of her. She is probably in shock, and when people are in shock, they don't act right. Their emotions and responses are not normal. Be patient with her. Lizzie needs time for all that has happened to settle."

I sat there for another minute or two, then pushed my chair back away from the table and stood up. "I guess I need to be going. Papa's expecting me at the store this afternoon to sweep the floor."

"I thought that was Maude's job," Mamaw asked as she walked me to the door. (Maude had been begging Papa for months to let her work at the store, and he finally allowed her to help him with the sweeping at the end of the day.)

"Yes, Ma'am, it is," I said. "But she is really having a hard time with Timothy's death. She didn't go to school today and probably won't go all week. She said she needed some time alone and didn't think she could sit through class all day. Papa told her that he understood and that she could stay home. I volunteered to help with the sweeping at the store. I felt so sorry for her."

Mamaw gave me a big hug and said, "Ollie, you are such a good big brother. She will appreciate this more than you will know."

"Papa told me to let Mr. Armstrong know Maude wouldn't be at school," I continued. "He's the new teacher. He came when Miss McCully got married and quit."

"Yes, I met him at church a few weeks ago," Mamaw said. "He seems to be a very nice young man. He's from somewhere up north and has such a funny accent."

"Yes, Ma'am," I said. "He's got a little stutter, too, and when he said 'Boston,' he sounded like an old sheep. 'Baa-baa-baa-stin.'"

Mamaw and I got a good laugh out of that. (As if we don't have our own 'funny' accent).

"Then there is Gussie," I said. "You know she started first grade two weeks ago, the day after Labor Day. She loves school; she doesn't talk about anything else. Even when Timothy so sick, all she wanted to do was to 'play school.' This morning she was so excited about going that she was up and ready before the chickens. Timothy's sickness and death don't seem to have had any effect on her."

"Ollie," Mamaw broke in, "you have to remember that Gussie is only six years old. She is not mature enough to grasp what has happened. She can be a handful at times, but she will be just fine."

That was one of the few times I remember my grandmother being wrong.

Chapter 14

It would be another four and a half years before Lizzie would have another child. During that time, Lizzie settled back into being mother and caregiver for my sisters and me, but she never mentioned Stephen and Timothy. It was as if those babies and those two years had never existed. She and Papa seemed to get along just fine, and she treated us very well. But she was different. She had changed. She seemed unusually happy. She had always enjoyed entertaining people, but now it seemed an obsession. She frequently invited friends over in the afternoon for coffee or tea and she was always talking about having a party. On Saturdays when Papa headed to Meridian for supplies, Lizzie would have a list of hats and dresses from the Sears and Roebuck catalogue that she wanted him to order as soon as he got to town. She said that she needed to look her best for any company that came by. I had never known her to order clothes; before she had always made them herself.

Lizzie also developed an interest in roses. But not just any rose; only white roses. This hobby started one hot Saturday in August when she decided to accompany Papa on one of his weekly trips to Meridian. She hadn't had a good visit with Aunt Florence in quite a while and felt this was as good a time as any to catch up on the happenings in Meridian. She and Aunt Florence were walking to town when they came upon "the most beautiful rosebush in the world." Lizzie just had to have some cuttings to take home. She rooted them and within a few years had a sizable rose garden.

The roses were very striking: soft pearl-white with a sweet, overpowering smell that would take your breath. The odor was very distinctive, almost pungent, but not unpleasant. It reminded me of some of the perfumes that many of the older women in church would wear; from a distance they were enjoyable, but you never wanted to sit beside them for an hour on a warm summer's day. Lizzie would spend hours babying her little chargers: watering, pampering, and pruning. From early summer to late fall every room in the house would be filled with her long-stemmed roses and their strange, intoxicating aroma. But the time would come when I wondered if her roses meant more to her than her own children.

During those four years Maude grew to be a little lady. At thirteen she was tall, slender, and was becoming a beauty, both inside and out. She reminded me so much of Mama—the same sweet smile, the same happy outlook on life, and the same love of people. She was smart, an excellent student, and had a knack for good conversation. People commented that she looked sixteen or seventeen.

Two years earlier, on Maude's eleventh birthday, Papa had bought her a piano. He had found it in Meridian and had it transported the ten miles to Lockhart by train. It was ancient and he said it wouldn't have survived the rough ride in a wagon. Before long she was quite an accomplished pianist. On Maude's thirteenth birthday, old Mrs. Matthews, the church pianist and Maude's piano teacher, proclaimed that she was retiring from her musical responsibilities at church, and from then on Maude was to be the official pianist at Lockhart Methodist Church.

And then there was Gussie. As Mamaw once said, "A real pistol." Unlike Maude, Gussie was not a scholar. Lizzie would say that getting her to study was like pulling teeth. It wasn't that she was dumb; she just had better things to do than study. She was always the center of attention at school, at home, and on the playground. Even at nine and ten years of age, Gussie was a heartbreaker. Every boy in school was, or had been, her sweetheart, wooed by her flashing eyelashes and pouty smile, only to have his heart dashed to the ground. She was moody and could fly off in a tantrum at the drop of a feather. She loved to dress up in Lizzie's new clothes and hats, and would parade around the house saying that when she grew up, she was going to marry a rich prince and live a life of luxury. Sadly, that would not happen.

During the summers of my fourteenth and fifteenth years, Junius, James, and I worked at the railroad depot. Papa had talked to Mr. Matthews, the depot manager (and also husband of the church pianist), who hired us to load and unload goods onto the box cars. It was hot and sweaty work. There is nothing more miserable than working in an enclosed area in the heat of a Mississippi summer. We would open up both sides of the box cars as we worked, trying to get some ventilation, but we still felt like we would roast.

I remember on one unusually hot and muggy afternoon, we were unloading fifty-pound bags of horse feed from a box car. We were sweating like race horses, and I felt like I was going to die. Junius stopped for a moment, wiped his brow, laughed, and said, "You know, I've made up my mind. I'm definitely going to church every Sunday for the rest of my life, because if Hell is anything like this box car, I want no part in it."

James and I laughed so hard we couldn't stand up.

When we had a few minutes break, I remember we would place pennies on the track and wait for trains to come by and flatten them out. Mamaw fussed at us and told us that we should be ashamed at wasting good money.

Fridays and Saturdays were usually the busiest days, and we would work from early morning to late afternoon. The other days of the week were fairly light; we would often be finished by noon and would head to the swimming hole at Ponta Creek.

I remember one Monday we were finished at noon and we were about to leave, when Mr. Matthews came to the loading dock and said that since it looked like Tuesday was going to be a slow day, we could take the day off. So James, Junius, and I packed up a supper and breakfast and headed to the creek to spend the night under the stars.

As we headed up the railroad tracks, we passed by Mr. Green's watermelon patch. The day was hot, and those big melons looked awfully good. Junius stopped in the middle of the tracks, pointed to the melon patch, and said, "I dare you to steal one of those watermelons. Ole Mr. Green wouldn't miss one little melon. There are plenty more."

James and I looked at each other, grinned impishly, and then took the dare. We slid down the railroad embankment and crawled under the fence. We found a nice, ripe melon, rolled it under the fence, and picked it up and ran. When we got to the creek, we busted that melon wide open and devoured the sweet, red meat. In ten minutes the only thing left was the rind.

After we finished, we laid down in the shade by the creek and rested; my belly felt like it was going to pop. After a few minutes, I started thinking about what we had done. I had never stolen anything in my life, and I had stolen something that I could easily have paid for with money I had made working. I thought what would Papa or Mamaw think of me? What would my Sunday school teacher think? Guilt suddenly overwhelmed me. I shared my feelings with Junius and James, and to my surprise, they both said that they were having the same guilty thoughts.

James stood up and said, "We need to go to Mr. Green right now and make things right. I won't to be able to sleep until my sins are forgiven."

Without hesitation, we got up, walked back to Mr. Green's front door, told him that we had stolen the melon, apologized, asked for forgiveness, and paid him a quarter. With our heavy burden of sin lifted from our souls, we headed back to Ponta Creek. Life was again good.

The next two summers, when I was sixteen and seventeen, I worked inside the depot office; Junius and James were still loading and unloading those wooden sweat boxes. One day, I started playing with the telegraph and found that I had a knack for Morse code. Before long I was sending and receiving messages faster than anyone else in the office, and having fun doing it. This love I developed with Samuel Morse's dots and dashes would one day become my livelihood and profession. Even though Alexander Graham Bell uttered those famous words "Mr. Watson, come here, I need you," on March 10, 1876, it would be well into the twentieth century before the telegraph would lose out to the telephone.

In the early summer of 1895, Lizzie started to have bouts of sickness and nausea again. Soon, Papa announced that Lizzie was with child and would probably have a baby in January. Maude was overjoyed, and couldn't wait. Gussie rolled her eyes; she couldn't care less.

On January 27, 1896, four and a half years after Timothy's death, Hugh Lee Parker was born. Lizzie was twenty-seven; I was eighteen, in my last year of school; Maude was thirteen; and Gussie, eleven. Papa was forty-three.

Hugh Lee was a happy healthy baby, similar to little Stephen. For some reason instead of calling him by his first name, Hugh, Maude started calling him "Hugh Lee," and before long everyone was doing the same.

Neighbors, many of whom said they had been praying for the past four years that God would send another baby to our household, came by to "ooh and aah" over the new arrival. They were happy for Papa and Lizzie, and pleased that a "bundle of happiness" had finally come that would "bring joy back to our sad home." And Lizzie loved showing off the new baby. She enjoyed entertaining and seemed to thrive on the attention.

She was a good mother to little Hugh Lee. In fact, Hugh Lee was blessed to have *two* good mothers: Lizzie and Maude. When Maude came home from school, she would take over most of the responsibilities of caring for the baby, except the breast feeding, of course. Gussie, who had taken such an interest in Stephen and Timothy, didn't pay much attention to Hugh Lee at all. She was too absorbed in her own little world. But Hugh Lee was a happy baby and didn't pay her much attention either.

In May of that year, I finished school and was hired full time at the depot. This was the beginning of my life as a telegrapher. I continued to live at home as I saw no reason to hurry out of our big house. I would stay at home for several more years, until I was married at the age of thirty-one.

For the next year life settled down again. Papa and I went to work; Maude and Gussie went to school; and Lizzie stayed home caring for Hugh Lee and entertaining the neighbors. And Mamaw was down the road in her little cottage. Even though I was now out of school, I never outgrew my afternoon visits with my grandmother, or her wonderful pies.

Chapter 15

On a cold, windy day in January 1897, I made one of my usual afternoon visits. Pecan pie was waiting.

"How was work today?" Mamaw asked as she lifted a large slice of pie out of its warm dish. "You want some coffee with your pie?"

"Yes, Ma'am, that would be great." I took my overcoat off and sat down at the table. "I need something to help warm me up: I just about froze coming home. As cold as it is, and with the clouds coming in, I wouldn't be surprised if it snowed tonight."

"I hope you're wrong. We don't need another snowstorm." She sat down beside me and poured us both a cup of coffee.

"This really hits the spot," I said as I tasted pie that would rival the finest restaurants in the country. "Mamaw, I don't see how you do it. You always have perfect tasting pecan pie. What's your secret?"

"It's good mature trees and years of experience," she replied with a big smile. "The first few pies I baked for your grandfather were nothing to brag about, but with trial and error, and a little help from his mother, I was able to come up with a fairly respectable pie."

"Respectable?" I remarked. "Mamaw, this is delicious!"

"Those trees at the old home place were planted by your grandfather over fifty years ago and have never failed to give a good crop. Hopefully you and your family will be picking up those pecans for another fifty years." She shook her head and glanced over at me. "That is, if you find a wife and have a family."

"Come on, Mamaw, I'm only nineteen years old. Give me a little time. Besides, I'm not ready for a family; but I am ready for another piece of this pie!"

Mamaw proudly served me another piece and asked, "Any interesting news come through on that telegraph machine today?"

"Yes, Ma'am. William McKinley was inaugurated today as the twenty-fifth president," I answered between savory bites. "According to the wire, there was a huge crowd in Washington for all the festivities. It was cold and rainy, but the Mall was packed."

"Can you believe that a good-for-nothing Republican is in the White House?" she remarked. "To think that he beat our 'man of the common people,' Mr. William Jennings Bryan. "You know that McKinley won because of all that rich northern money."

"Maybe so," I said, "but President Cleveland and the Democratic Party haven't been able to get the economy going after the stock market crash of ninety-three. It didn't matter that the crash occurred only a few months after he took office. He got the blame anyway, and the Democrats have suffered for it. The Republicans are really sweeping up all the elections. Unemployment is still very high up north and people want something different."

"Well, I still think that Mr. Bryan could straighten things out in Washington."

"But he won't get the chance these four years." I added.

"Well, at least here in Mississippi we still have a Democrat as Governor," Mamaw said.

"By the way," she continued, changing the subject, "I was by the house visiting with Lizzie and Hugh Lee this morning. He's growing like a weed, and at a year old he's starting to get into everything. Lizzie said that since he started walking, she really has to keep an eye on him. She said that yesterday she lost sight of him for a few seconds, and before she knew it, he was in her knitting and had unraveled two days of work. It's so good to see Lizzie with Hugh Lee. Having a little one around has made her seem like her old self."

"Maybe so," I replied, "but she is not her old self. She is not the same. Since Timothy died . . . I don't know, I can't put my finger on it, but she just doesn't act the same. She does seem better now that Hugh Lee is here. She is good to him, but all her actions seem. . . ." I paused to find the right words, " . . . so superficial, almost like down deep she really doesn't care. She seems more interested in how she looks and how she is perceived by the neighbors. And those white roses. Sometimes she shows more attention to them than to the baby. Even now, in the dead of winter, she is out checking on them, making sure they are wrapped and don't freeze, while Maude takes care of Hugh Lee. Maude is more of a loving mother to him than Lizzie is."

Mamaw sat silently in thought for a moment and then said, "Ollie, I have to agree with you. Lizzie has changed, but I don't see how anyone can lose two babies and not change. She is also older now, and she has a more mature outlook than she did a few years ago. Lizzie does like to visit and entertain, and I think that's good for her. And everyone, including me, likes her quick wit and humor. She's going to be just fine, that is, unless she doesn't stop spending all of your father's money on those fancy hats. He told her that if she doesn't slow down, he is going to end up in debtor's prison." Mamaw laughed half-heartedly. "And she does have some of the prettiest roses I've ever seen."

I finished my pie and stood up. "I need to be running along. Maude and I have been working on a winter garden for the past few days, and we hope to have some carrots, turnips, and mustard greens by spring. We've finished most of the digging and tilling, and we want to get the seeds in the ground today. There is a full moon tonight, and we want our plants to get off to a good start."

I gave Mamaw a big hug and kissed her on the forehead. I smiled as I remembered that only a few years ago she was the one kissing me on the forehead.

Chapter 16

On May 26, 1897, Papa headed to Meridian on one of his usual Saturday trips to pick up supplies. It was a beautiful day for a trip to the city and I wanted to go with him, but I had to work all day at the station. School was about to let out for the summer and the girls weren't interested in sitting in a wagon for five hours on such a beautiful day (two and a half hours each way) and neither was Lizzie interested in packing up Hugh Lee for the long trip. So Papa made the trip alone. He had no big plans for the weekend and no reason to get back in a hurry, so he decided to stay the night with his brother, John, and come back Sunday afternoon.

Saturday afternoon and evening were uneventful. Mamaw joined us for supper and brought coconut cake for dessert. Coconuts were not commonly found at the general store in Lockhart, but when they did appear it was a must that Mamaw purchase one and make the best tasting coconut cake south of the Mason-Dixon Line.

When I was younger, I remember Mamaw gave me the honor of "harvesting" the meat of the coconut. First, I would drive a nail into one of the "eyes" of the coconut and then let the sweet liquor drip into a bowl. Mamaw would then divide the nectar in half, one half to be used to make the cake, the other half for us to drink. Next, I would bust that big nut wide open with a hammer and dig out the meat. The meat was then shredded and sprinkled on the icing of the cake. That icing was so sweet and moist that the bites would melt in your mouth.

That night after supper, while the girls did the dishes, Mamaw, Lizzie, Hugh Lee, and I sat on the porch and enjoyed the sounds and smells of the cool Mississippi night. Early on, as it was just getting dark, the "coo" of a dove dominated the twilight. As the sky continued to darken, the "coo" was soon replaced by the steady, monotonous serenade of the crickets and the frogs, with an occasional interruption by the "whoo-whoo" of an old owl. The sweet smell of honeysuckle was ever present and almost intoxicating. There's nothing like a cool evening on the front porch in the rural South.

Mamaw was on the porch swing holding Hugh Lee, swinging gently, the link chain squeaking in cadence. Hugh Lee was teething and was chewing on an old wooden spoon, happy and content as could be. In the darkness, the lightning bugs (they're called fireflies up North) made their flickering presence known. Maude and Gussie soon came out with a couple of Mason jars and filled them up with "at least a million" of the flashing bugs.

After the "gathering of the lights" Lizzie excused herself and little Hugh Lee. "It's getting late," she said. "Time to put the little one to bed. It's such a beautiful night, and I know ya'll could sit out here all night, but don't stay up too late. Tomorrow is Sunday, and I don't want any sleepy heads in church."

Mamaw, the girls, and I stayed on the porch for another thirty minutes and talked. The girls were so excited that summer was almost here and that homework would soon be gone. They were looking forward to the quiet, lazy days of summer.

"I'm glad we were able to get the garden in early this year," fourteen year old Maude said as she opened one of the Mason jars and watched the little flashing bugs escape. "Some of the tomatoes are already starting to ripen and should be ready in a week or two. And it looks like the snap peas and okra will be ready to pick early, too."

Gussie was sitting on the porch swing with Mamaw. "Maude, don't forget you promised to help me with sewing this summer," she exclaimed, as she swung her legs back and forth. "I hope to make at least three or four new dresses before fall. You know I'm going to be thirteen this year, and I want to look my best when school starts back."

After a few minutes, Mamaw stood up and said, "It's time for me go to bed, too. Sunday mornings do tend to come early." She kissed us all goodbye and headed down the road to her little cottage. The girls and I reluctantly went inside to bed.

That night I didn't sleep well at all. I tossed and turned and I never could get comfortable. Though it was a long time ago, I faintly remember having disturbing dreams. I can't remember any of the details, but they were dreams that left me feeling that things weren't right; that things were undone, incomplete. In the early hours of Sunday morning, I finally drifted into a deep sleep.

About six-thirty in the morning, I suddenly awoke, confused, disoriented. Someone was screaming. I jumped out of bed and ran down the stairs. The screaming was coming from the nursery. I opened the door and there stood Lizzie, with Hugh Lee in her arms. My heart was pounding out of my chest as a walked over to them. I touched his skin. It was cold, lifeless. Hugh Lee Parker had died during the night. He was sixteen months old.

When I look back at the many times of grief in my life, that moment, that instant when I realized that Hugh Lee was dead, was the most sickening, horrible feeling that I can recall. Until that time of grief, I had always had at least a little time to prepare. With Mama, Stephen, and Timothy, there had been a time of sickness: time that allowed me to ready myself for the worst. With

Mama it had only been a day, but it was a day: a day of readying my heart to accept death. Or more than accepting death, it was a time of watching life slip away. With Hugh Lee there was no preparation; just instant death. The sudden shock that it was over, that there was no time to pray, no time to plead, no time to bargain with God.

That afternoon, I left family and friends who had gathered at the house and headed down the road toward Meridian to meet Papa. I stopped two hundred yards from the house, sat on a fallen tree, and waited. Soon Papa arrived and I gave him the terrible news. He slowly stood up, got out of the wagon, came over, and sat down beside me. We sat there, talked, and cried for an hour. We then went home.

Two days later, on May 29, 1897, Hugh Lee Parker was buried in Lockhart Cemetery. We gathered at the house afterwards to grieve and receive visitors.

At dark, I walked my grandmother home. We walked silently, but I could tell my grandmother was deeply troubled. As we approached her house, she sighed and said, "Death from old age I understand. Disease and accidents I try to understand. But to just die. A baby, happy and healthy. Not even a sniffle or a cold. God, please give me an answer!"

That night was one of the few times I saw my grandmother wrestle with God. Her faith was so strong. Whatever the circumstances, her faith and trust would always carry her through. But that night she was struggling. I remember her questioning God, pleading for an answer.

"God, are You dealing with us as You dealt with Job? Are You stripping us bare, taking away everything that we hold dear to see if we will break? How much more can we take?" She paused and looked up at the star-filled heavens. "But, then do we have a right to question God at all?"

She thought of what God had spoken to Job, "Who is this that darkeneth counsel by words without knowledge? . . . Where wast thou when I laid the foundations of the earth? Declare if thou hast understanding."(Job 38: 2, 4)

How can we ever understand how powerful and almighty God really is?

"I don't understand it, but I have to trust that God is ultimately in control. That He ultimately has our best interest at heart," Mamaw affirmed. "There can be no other way."

It is not the patience of Job that we should remember, but his faith.

We walked on to her house and sat silently on the porch. After a few minutes Mamaw softly spoke. "Poor Maude, she has taken this so hard. She hasn't stopped crying, and she has hardly eaten anything in two days. She was such a good, loving big sister to Hugh Lee. As you said in the past, she was really a second mother to him. She is so heartbroken. And day after tomorrow is her birthday."

"Yes, Ma'am," I said. "She will be fifteen."

"Fifteen," she pondered. "Why, at that age I was already married to your grandfather, and your Uncle John was on the way. My, my, times have changed. Most girls don't get married now until they are nineteen or twenty. Maude is such a mature young lady for her age. Some day she will make such a good wife and mother."

In time Maude did become a wonderful wife and a loving mother to three sons and a daughter. But for a while, we worried that she would be an old maid; she did not marry until she was twenty-eight.

"It's not going to be a happy birthday for her. But I'll make her a strawberry cake. The strawberries are good and ripe right now, and hopefully she will enjoy it."

"Mamaw," I said, "Lizzie's not acting normal. It's like after Timothy died. Except for Sunday morning when she was screaming and crying as she held Hugh Lee, I don't think she has shed a single tear. I can't see any evidence of grief. Today has been almost like one of her parties, entertaining the neighbors, serving cookies and tea cakes. She seems to be more concerned about how her hat looks on her than the fact that she has just lost another child. And another thing. Last night while she was straightening up the house, she said that it's a shame it was not a few weeks later. The roses would be blooming and she would be able to show them off to the neighbors. Mamaw, I don't understand it."

"Ollie, it's hard for me to understand, too. But this must be her way of dealing with this tragedy," Mamaw replied. "It's her way of coping, acting like it didn't happen, blocking it out of her mind. It doesn't seem right or even healthy, but what can we do? We can't make her grieve the way we think she should. We just have to let things run their course."

"Mamaw, that night when Hugh Lee died, I didn't sleep well. I don't know what it was, but I kept having strange dreams, like something wasn't right. I faintly remember that in the dreams something was going on in the house, someone was up and moving around. And the more I think about those dreams, the more I wonder if I was really dreaming. I can't get that thought out of my head."

Mamaw shifted in her chair and said, "When we grieve we sometimes don't think straight. The sadness muddles our thoughts. And trying to make sense of dreams is like trying to grasp a mirage. It is always just out of your reach. And as far as a feeling that things are going on in the house during the night, I often have that feeling, and I live alone; the wind, the creaking of those old walls. The mind plays tricks on us, especially when we have a fitful night and can't sleep."

"Maybe so," I said, "but I still don't feel right about it."

"How is Gussie doing?" Mamaw asked.

"Mamaw, that girl is twelve years old, but just doesn't seem to grasp what has happened, or either she doesn't care. She is so wrapped up in her own little world that Hugh Lee's death seems to have had no effect at all on her. Is she ever going to grow up?'"

"Give her some time. She is a bit immature and maybe a little spoiled, but she'll be okay; she'll grow up. But for now, she is the baby again."

Chapter 17

Gussie was not the baby again for long. Two months later Papa and Lizzie again announced that there was going to be another baby. Seven months later, on February 1, 1898, Lizzie's fourth son, Roger Lloyd Parker, was born. I was twenty, Maude was fifteen, and Gussie was thirteen.

Sadly, I don't remember a lot about Roger's life. He lived only nineteen months. He was the fourth of my five little brothers to live a very short life and then die; his life just kind of blended in with the others. His time on earth seemed so uneventful, so unmemorable. I feel guilty saying it, but I can't even remember what he looked like. But I remember his death like it was yesterday.

On the morning of Friday, September 6, 1899, I caught the early morning train to Meridian to purchase some office supplies for the depot. The station manager, Mr. Matthews, had never liked going to the "big city." He said that the noise and crowds gave him the shakes, and it wouldn't hurt his feelings at all to never leave Little Lockhart again. And he never did. Six months later he died in his sleep and was buried in Lockhart Cemetery.

I soon became the official "depot delegate" whenever someone needed to go to Meridian. But I didn't mind; I enjoyed my quick little trips.

Meridian was rapidly growing, and for several years it had been the largest city in Mississippi, now with close to 25,000 inhabitants. There were plenty of shops to browse through. The "Gay Nineties" of the Northeast had finally touched our little city and I got a kick out of seeing all the funny bright new clothes that the young men and women "of means" were wearing. I also never missed a stop at Felix Weidmann's Restaurant and Soda Fountain for a glass of bubbly Coca-Cola.

Mid-afternoon I boarded the train with my load of supplies. When I arrived back at Lockhart, Mamaw was standing on the platform waiting for me. She obviously had been crying; her eyes were red and swollen.

"Ollie, there has been an accident. Roger has been hurt. You need to come home now. I've talked to Mr. Matthews and he said he would get the supplies unloaded from the train for you."

"What happened?" I asked immediately. I felt faint and could feel my heart beating in my throat.

"A pot of scalding water fell on Roger in the kitchen. He's in very bad shape. Dr. Knox was two miles out in the country helping with a difficult childbirth when it happened. When your Papa finally found him, he couldn't come immediately. Dr. Knox asked if Roger was crying. Papa told him that he didn't cry at all, and that when he had left the house, little Roger was just quivering. Dr. Knox shook his head and said that was not good; it sounded like a bad burn to him. He told Papa to wrap him up in a blanket and he would be there as soon as he could. When I left the house to come get you, Dr. Knox had just arrived. He said it looked very bad."

Roger Lloyd Parker died that afternoon and was buried two days later in Lockhart Cemetery. He was nineteen months old. He was laid to rest beside three brothers whom he never knew: Stephen, Timothy, and Hugh Lee.

The Reverend Lewis, minister of Lockhart Methodist Church, conducted the ceremony, as he had done three times before. His words of comfort had changed little. His sermon for the dead and those left behind was straight from the *Book of Common Prayer.* At the end of the service he added, "We do not understand all the ways of the Lord. We do not understand why he takes back the precious, as with these innocent little boys. But we know that God is in control, and what has happened is the will of God. It is His will to take them home to be with Him.

Chapter 18

The day after the funeral was Labor Day, a new holiday which had recently been put into effect. And I was relieved that I didn't have to go to work. I needed time to grieve and to sort things out. After lunch I headed over to Mamaw's house to talk.

"Ollie, come on in," Mamaw said as she heard the old front steps creak. "Do you want some pie?"

"No, Ma'am," I answered. "I'm not very hungry today. Why don't we sit outside on the swing. It's a little too warm to be inside this afternoon."

"It has been pretty hot today," she replied as she opened the screen door and came outside. "I haven't been very hungry today either." She sat down beside me and continued. "I'm still so upset with Reverend Lewis' message at the funeral yesterday. 'God's will.' That's what he said. It was 'God's will' that Roger should die. It was 'God's will' that Stephen and Timothy and Hugh Lee should die. I don't believe that. Yes, God is in control, but there's a big difference in what God allows to happen and what He 'wills' to happen. I don't have all the answers, but I know the Bible says that His will is that 'none should perish.'"

"Mamaw, tell me what happened on Friday with Roger," I interrupted. "I haven't been able to get a good answer. Everyone is too upset to talk about it."

"Ollie, my story is pretty sketchy right now, but this is how I've pieced it together. You know that school starts tomorrow, and on Friday the girls were working on some new dresses for school. They wanted to get them finished before settling in to another year of lessons. That morning Maude took a break from sewing and went out to the garden to pick some corn and butter beans. Gussie was in the house sewing some lace on one of the dresses that she and Maude had almost finished. Lizzie had put a big pot of water on the stove to boil for the corn.

"According to what I understand, Gussie was watching Roger and Lizzie had stepped out on the back porch to cool off. It was hot that day and boiling water will drive you out of the kitchen in no time, especially when you're five months pregnant like Lizzie is." (Yes, Lizzie was pregnant again for the fifth time.)

"It was so hot in the kitchen that Lizzie decided not to go back inside until Maude came back with the corn, so she walked down to her rose garden to prune and water. No one knows what happened next, but you know how active and mobile that little fellow had gotten to be, getting into everything. Well, somehow Roger got into the kitchen and before anyone could do anything, he had turned the pot of boiling water on top of himself.

"Maude came down the road to my house, screaming at the top of her lungs, told me what had happened, and ran on to get Papa. When I got to the house Lizzie was holding him; he wasn't making a sound, limp as a rag doll."

"Mamaw," I said, "I just don't understand. It doesn't make sense to me. How in the world could that little fellow have turned that pot over? There is no way he could have reached it and absolutely no way he could have hit the stove hard enough to make it turn over. That stove is cast iron and weighs a ton. I tried to shake it this morning and that stove won't budge. There was no chair near the stove for him to climb on. It just makes no sense."

"Your Papa initially said the same thing, but then he said that there was a broom lying on the floor beside the stove. He said that it looked like the broom had been propped up beside the stove, and Roger must have knocked it down, hitting the handle on the pot. That has to be what happened."

I shook my head and said, "It still doesn't make sense."

Mamaw looked at me with a shocked expression. "What are you saying?"

"I'm not saying anything," I answered. "I just don't understand."

"Well, we are all still in a state of shock right now and it's hard for any of us to understand," Mamaw said. "We may never be able to put it all together and get a good answer, but there is no question in my mind that it was an accident. To think otherwise would be horrible."

"Tell me where Gussie was when it happened," I asked.

"She said that she was in the parlor working on a dress, watching the baby. She said that she got distracted, trying to make the lace fit just right, and the next thing she knew, there was a noise and a splash in the kitchen. She ran into the kitchen and started screaming for Lizzie."

"Gussie should have been more responsible. She's fourteen years old. She ought to know better than to let a baby run around unattended."

"Ollie, it won't do any good trying to place blame. It won't bring Roger back. Gussie made a mistake; I think she realizes that. We all get distracted at times from what we are supposed to do."

I remember thinking to myself, "A mistake? Distracted? My God, a child died!" And if Gussie was remorseful, she was sure hiding it.

Chapter 19

As had happened after Stephen's death, Dr. Knox put Lizzie to bed. According to him the stress was too much for her, and he didn't want her going into labor. She did well, receiving guests in her bedroom. She seemed to be in her element, sitting in the middle of the bed, pillows propping her up, with friends and family ready to help with every need.

Four months later, on February 4, 1900, Eugenia Parker was born, the first of two little girls to brighten our home for a short time. Lizzie was thirty-one; I was twenty-two; Maude seventeen; and Gussie fifteen. Papa was forty-six.

Gena, as we called her, was a good, happy baby. For her first few months, Maude, her oldest half sister, was her mother in almost every way, except for supplying the milk.

I was now into my fourth year as telegrapher at the depot, and thoroughly enjoyed my work. In April, old Mr. Matthews died in his sleep. He had been station manager of the Lockhart Depot for almost twenty years. He was laid to rest in Lockhart Cemetery. His wife, long time pianist for the church and piano teacher for almost everyone in the community who had ever taken lessons, was soon to follow. Within six months she too would die and join her husband in Lockhart Cemetery.

Soon after Mr. Matthews' death, I was promoted by the M & O Railroad to take his place as station manager. For a young twenty-two year old, this was a lot of responsibility, and as I look back, more responsibility than I should have taken on. I feel that I did a fairly good job. However, there were times when I needed some free advice and encouragement from my wise grandmother.

On May 1, 1900, I stopped by Mamaw's cottage as I had almost every afternoon for the past fourteen years.

"Well how is the new station manager doing after one week on the job?" Mamaw asked, with a little hint of pride in her voice for her grandson. "You want some peaches? They're so ripe they will melt in your mouth."

"Thanks, I'd love one," I answered. "But don't peel it. You know how I love to eat the whole thing, fuzzy peel and all.

"Everything is going well," I remarked between juicy bites, "but I did have to lay down the law today. I think some of the loaders are trying to test the limits with their new boss, trying to see how much they can get away with. This afternoon J. E. King, who has been loading for about two years, disappeared for about an hour. Didn't say 'excuse me' or 'kiss my foot'; he just disappeared. When he showed back up, I asked him where he had been. He said he had some business to take care of. You know, the thought of him doing something like that when Mr. Matthews was alive, why, J. E. would have been thrown out on his ear, no questions asked, and he knows it. But he's a really good worker, and I don't want to lose him. So I suspended him without pay for a week and made it very plain that if he or anyone else pulled such a stunt again, there would not be a second chance."

Mamaw thought for a minute and said, "I think you did fine. They are just trying you. But if it happens again, do as you said. Fire him on the spot, good worker or not. You have to make everyone know that you mean business. By the way, are you still handling that telegraph, or have you delegated that to someone else?"

"I plan on continuing the telegraph. No one else at the station can catch the dots and dashes as well as I can. I don't mean to brag, but it's just so easy for me. I've found I can do them in my head, and I don't even have to write them down. Coding is the most fun I have at work.

"Talking about the telegraph," I continued, "we got a sad message today on the wire. Do you remember that engineer on the M & O railroad named John Jones? The one they called 'Casey,' who used to run the route between Meridian and Jackson, Tennessee.

"Casey Jones," Mamaw pondered. "Was he the fellow who was so tall, about 6'5", if I remember correctly? If he's the one I'm thinking about, he was such a nice engineer. When he would stop in Lockhart, everybody enjoyed talking with him."

"Yes, Ma'am, that's him. We received a wire today that he was killed early yesterday morning in a train collision at Vaughan, Mississippi."

"How horrible!" Mamaw gasped. "What happened?"

"A few years back he transferred from the M & O to the Illinois Central Railroad and started making the Cannonball run between Chicago and New Orleans. I remember that when he was still on the M & O, he was always a stickler for staying on schedule. He was very nice, but hated to be late. I was still working on the loading dock back then, when he would stop in Lockhart, and he was always pushing us to hurry and get loaded. He had to get going or he would be late.

"Night before last, according to the wire report, Casey had finished up a northbound run to Memphis. He was about to sign out and go get some sleep, when the engineer who was supposed to take the run back south to Canton reported in sick. Casey agreed to make the five-hour run. Well, the train, a passenger service, was already ninety-five minutes behind schedule, and left Memphis yesterday morning at 12:50 A.M. The wire says that he was making up the time, going as fast as seventy miles per hour when he reached Vaughan, about fifteen miles north of Canton. Apparently there was a freight train stalled on the track, and Casey ran right into it. The wire states that when he realized what was about to happen, he began to brake as hard as he could and told his fireman to jump for his life. Casey was the only one killed. Not a single passenger was injured. If he hadn't stayed with the train, no telling how many would have been killed."

"How sad," Mamaw said with amazement. She then shook her head and remarked, "Whenever I ride on a train, which isn't very often, I'm always scared to death that something bad is going to happen, and that story doesn't help a bit. When a train goes its normal speed, it seems so unnatural. But to be going seventy miles an hour! That's just unbelievable! Our bodies were not meant to travel that fast. Why, at that speed I would suspect that we would start falling apart!"

John "Casey" Jones would be immortalized as the most famous railroad engineer of all time thanks to a tune made up by Wallace Saunders, a colored engine "wiper" in Canton. He had a knack for making up songs and "The Ballad of Casey Jones" was soon being sung up and down the Illinois Central. The song was picked up by two vaudeville performers, Frank and Bert Leighton, and the rest is history. Sadly, neither Casey's widow nor Wallace Saunders ever received a penny from the song. *"Come all you 'rounders if you want to hear / A story 'bout a brave engineer, / Casey Jones was the 'rounder's name / 'Twas on the Illinois Central that he won his fame."*

"How is Gena doing?" Mamaw asked. "It's hard to believe that she will be three months old in another few days."

"She's doing fine, getting bigger every day. You know she's been a night owl, sleeping through the day and awake all night, but she finally started sleeping through the night this week. I remember that all of the other babies were sleeping all night when they were six weeks old, except for sickly little Timothy, so it's been a struggle. But now everyone is getting a good night's sleep.

"Mamaw," I continued, "Lizzie may be the birth mother for that little girl, but Maude is the *real* mother. She seems to do everything for that baby: changes her, bathes her, rocks her. The only thing that Lizzie does for Gena is nurse her. I would suspect that Maude would be doing that, too, if she could."

"Maude is such a natural mother," Mamaw responded. "She loves babies so much. And Lizzie just lets her do what she wants, and that is being a mother to Gena. You know this is the first little girl since Gussie was born."

"Yes, Ma'am, but things are fixing to change," I remarked. "You know Maude graduates from school in three weeks and has decided to go to college. She will be enrolling in Meridian Female College and moving to Meridian in August. And after she's gone, I don't know what Lizzie's going to do. We both know that Gussie is no help at all with the baby or with the chores. Mamaw, I bet you will be enlisted into service."

"I knew Maude was talking about college," Mamaw said. "And since she doesn't have any young fellow courting her, I think that's wonderful. She is so smart; such a wonderful little lady. No one else in our family has been to college, and I'm so proud of her. And it's so good that your father has done well enough in business to be able to afford it. But I do hope a husband for her shows up soon. Ollie, you know that you could go to college if you wanted. You're a smart fellow, too."

"No thanks, I'll stay where I am and enjoy my 'dots and dashes.' The idea of study doesn't interest me at all."

Chapter 20

Maude enrolled in college and left Lockhart that summer. She focused her studies on music and history. (The music studies would be of great value in the years to come. Maude would one day become the pianist at Hawkins Memorial Methodist Church.) She came home to Lockhart on occasion, but for the most part she stayed at school. With Maude gone, care of little Gena fell back on Lizzie. Whether it was that Lizzie now found it overwhelming to care for a baby or she just didn't have any interest in the day-to-day needs of a baby anymore, I don't really know. But another member of the family was added that summer.

Octavia was a forty-year-old colored woman whose husband had died a few years back. For the past year she had been working for a family in Meridian, but the family fell on hard times and had to let her go. Uncle John, Papa's brother, heard about her and put her in touch with Papa. She was more than happy to move to our little community and help us out.

Octavia came to live with us and became a nanny to little Gena and a cook, cleaning lady, and overall head of the house for the rest of us. I know that Mamaw would have been more than glad to fill the position, but she was getting older and her knees and hips were beginning to slow her down. She realized that her time for caring for a family, and especially for a baby, had passed.

Octavia was an interesting woman. She had grown up in Meridian, the only child of a very attractive, slender colored woman who had never worked, but always seemed to have plenty of money and nice clothes. Octavia said that her mother had "friends" in high places in Meridian.

Octavia grew up having everything she needed, within reason for a little colored girl. But when Octavia was in her mid teens, her mother was killed under very strange circumstances: shot in the back of the head late one night in one of the well-to-do white areas of town. The murder was kept quiet and never made the paper. Rumors floated around for a few weeks, but no one seemed to know the real story. Octavia never discussed the details of her mother's death.

Octavia had no other relatives and the death of her mother left her alone. But within a few months she married and settled in one of the nicer colored neighborhoods in Meridian. She and her husband had one son, a very bright young man who excelled in school and went on to college. When she came to work for us, her son was attending Meharry Medical College in Nashville, Tennessee, and would later graduate with honors and become a physician in the Nashville area.

One day Octavia was talking about family and Meridian and let it slip that her father was a well-respected, married white businessman in Meridian. He and her mother had been "friends" for years. He had been very good to her and her mother, and even after her mother's death, had continued to provide for her. He had died a few years ago and left provisions to educate her son. But when money ran out, she found it necessary to find employment.

Octavia was smart as a whip and essentially ran the house. What she said went, no questions asked. She was an excellent cook; her pies rivaled Mamaw's (but I would *never* voice it out loud; it would have put Mamaw in her grave). She was also a

The Parker Family, Circa 1915

Lockhart Methodist Church

Stephen's first wife, Cornelia, and *the Angels of Lockhart*

Stephen Decatur Parker
"Papa"

Elizabeth Bludworth Parker
"Lizzie"

Clelia Maude Parker Coburn
"Maude"

Mary Augusta Parker Jarman Williams
"Gussie"

This is the only known picture of one of *the Angels of Lockhart*

meticulous housekeeper, but she expected us to do our part. When Gussie would leave clothes lying around, Octavia wasn't about to pick them up; she would find Gussie, march her in, and stand over her until she picked up every piece.

We all fell in love with Octavia and her take-command personality. Gena adored her, and she adored Gena, and Octavia soon became her new "mother," taking over the day-to-day loving care that had previously been given by Maude.

Lizzie also loved having Octavia around. She had lost interest in housekeeping over the past couple of years, but continued to enjoy entertaining and tending to her roses. Octavia always had the house spotless and had a steady supply of cookies and cakes for anyone who happened by.

Papa was engrossed in his business and seemed to be spending more and more time with his work. I continued to run the depot and to see the world through those little dots and dashes. Gussie, at age fifteen, had developed into a beauty and was breaking the hearts of every young man at school. Lizzie was busy trying to make herself the social center of our little community. Octavia was the ruler and Gena was her little princess. And of course there was Mamaw, slowly growing older.

Chapter 21

The next summer, the summer of 1901, was rather mild and wet. Throughout the entire months of June and July, we were blessed with late afternoon thundershowers and cool breezes that made life at this usually muggy, hot, stagnant time of year almost enjoyable. The temperatures were rarely above the mid eighties and the lows at night were in the sixties. With the pleasant wet weather came a bumper crop of fruits and berries. The blackberry vines and blueberry bushes were sagging almost to the ground with the extra weight of their plump, juicy treasures. The fig trees were so full of fruit that we didn't mind sharing a few of them with the blue jays and mockingbirds.

Late one Sunday afternoon in early July, we were sitting on the front porch enjoying the beautiful weather when Mamaw said, "Why don't we head down to the far end of the pasture and pick some more blackberries before it gets dark. I was by there a few days ago and there were so many unripe, red berries that it looked like the vines were on fire. By now they ought to be nice and ripe."

I shook my head and asked, "Do we really need anymore blackberries? I'm still itching from last week when we picked a gallon of them closer to the house. Those chiggers ate me alive!"

"Whatever you want to do," Mamaw said. "I was wanting to make sure we have enough berries to last us through the winter."

With a shrug of her shoulders she continued, "But if you don't want to enjoy my delicious, mouthwatering blackberry cobbler year round, that's okay with me."

I stood up and said, "Mamaw, you talked me into it. I'll get a couple of buckets, and let's go!"

With the weather so nice, not a rain cloud in the sky, Octavia decided to join us. She said she needed the exercise.

"I'll join you, too," Lizzie said as she reached for her pruning shears. "The walk will do me good, but first I need to tend to my roses. With all the rain, the blooms are more beautiful than ever, but the moisture has caused some of the leaves to develop brown spots. I'll catch up with ya'll when I finish pruning."

Papa had some work to do in town and Gussie was left to look after seventeen month old Gena.

Mamaw was right about the berries. There were more ripe blackberries than you could imagine. In less than an hour we had picked over three gallons, more than enough to last through the year. Lizzie joined us shortly before we finished.

As the sun began to set, we headed back across the pasture. The weather was cool and quiet with just a hint of a breeze. The only noise was the shuffle of our shoes through the tall grass and the occasional croak of a frog from the pond. It was one of those times when you wish that life would stand still forever.

As we approached the house, Gussie was sitting on the front steps of the house, reading a book, engrossed in the story with her nose almost touching the pages.

"That must be a very interesting book you're reading," Mamaw said.

"Yes, Ma'am, it is," Gussie replied. "I was reading in the parlor, but it's gotten too dark to see well inside. I'm in a very exciting chapter and came outside to read while there is still light."

"I've never known you to enjoy reading," Lizzie said. "Maybe you'll be this interested in your school books when classes start back in the fall."

"Where's Gena?" Mamaw asked.

Gussie looked up from her book with a puzzled look on her face and answered, "She's in the parlor playing with one of her dolls. I'll go check on her."

Gussie stood up, placed her book on the porch swing, and walked to the screen door. She strained to look in the dark house and called, "Gena, where are you?" There was no sound from the house. Gussie opened the door and walked in. A few moments later she came back, the puzzled look was now one of panic. "I can't find her. The last time I saw her she was sitting on the floor in the parlor as happy as could be playing with her dolls, but she's not there now."

We all rushed into the house and looked everywhere: under the beds, in all the dressers and wardrobes, in every closet and corner. But there was no Gena. I went to the back door and found the door was unlatched. The back porch was quiet, no baby in sight. About this time Papa came in and asked what was going on. Gena was lost and we could not find her.

We headed outside; it was almost dark and becoming difficult to see. We spread out in the yard, calling out as we searched. Nothing. Everyone was beginning to panic: Mamaw and Octavia began to cry, wondering where their little baby could be. Lizzie shook her head and said, "I hope she didn't wander down to the pond. She could very well be at the bottom right now. And if she is, it is all Gussie's fault."

Papa looked at her sternly, and said, "Lizzie, be quiet. We will have no more talk like that. Don't waste time and keep looking."

Papa and I went back into the house and brought out all the lanterns that we could find. Papa laid out a plan. "Mother, you and Octavia head north on the road, and Lizzie, you head south. As you look, tell as many neighbors as you can and ask them to help. Ollie, you and Gussie go look around the barn and then down in the pasture. She may have tried to follow you when you went berry picking. I'll head down to the pond."

I felt a shiver when he mentioned the pond. Please, God! Please don't let him find little Gena in the pond!

As Gussie and I searched, I didn't say a word. I knew that if I did, my words would not be pleasant. I was burning with anger and with panic. How in the world could Gussie be the way she was? Did she not ever think about anything but herself and her own little world? Would she ever learn to be responsible? Was this going to be a repeat of Roger's death—"a mistake, distraction?" I prayed with all my heart. Please, God, please let Gena be okay.

Fifteen minutes later I heard Mamaw and Octavia yelling. They had found her, and she was okay. Gena was sitting on the front porch steps of Mamaw's little cottage. Apparently, she had wandered out of the house and up the road, recognized Mamaw's house, and just sat down and waited. She had her little doll with her and seemed happy and untroubled. We were relieved that she was okay. Lizzie, however, was more interested in telling Gussie how irresponsible she had been.

After that incident, Gussie was never left alone to look after Gena again; Mamaw and Octavia made sure of that. They didn't want anything to happen to Gena. Sadly, they would not be successful.

Chapter 22

Three months later, in late October, Octavia received a telegraph from Meridian. It was a simple note: "COME HOME, STOP, IMPORTANT BUSINESS, STOP." That was it, nothing more. When I gave it to her that evening, she read it slowly, and a puzzled look came over her face. The only thing she said was that she needed to catch the train in the morning and would be back in a couple of days. We had no idea what it was about and Octavia offered no clue.

At dinner that night, a Thursday night, Papa said that he had planned to go to Meridian on Saturday, but that he would be glad to make his run a day early, and save Octavia half of her train fare. She was very thankful, and the next morning they headed out in the wagon for Meridian.

The weather in October in central Mississippi is more unpredictable than a cat. The day started out pleasant, warm, and a little muggy. By early afternoon the wind began to blow from the northwest, and the air began to cool rapidly. Within an hour the sky darkened, and it started to rain a cold, bone chilling rain that was not going to stop any time soon. At the station I received a wire from Papa saying that, because of the storm, he was going to stay the night in Meridian with his brother and come home on Saturday.

It rained all night. The claps of thunder shook the house and rattled the windows, and the lightening was almost blinding. Sleep was difficult for all of us, and several times through the night I vaguely remember hearing Gena cry out when the thunder was especially loud. Reminiscent of a night four years earlier, my sleep was fitful and interrupted by strange dreams: dreams in which things were undone, not right. I remember little Gena was crying and someone was with her, holding her close. In my dream it was Mama, not Lizzie, but my *real* mother who was comforting her. Mama was whispering to Gena not to cry, that she would take care of her; that there was no need to be afraid, because little Gena was very special, more special than anything else in the world.

Sometime during the early morning, the rain stopped, and our world was silent and still again. I awoke shortly after daybreak. The sky had cleared and there was a fresh coolness in the air. The house was quiet, unusually quiet. I dressed and went downstairs. As I reached the lower steps, I suddenly froze, horrified at what I saw. In the hall in front of the nursery stood Lizzie holding Gena, rocking her gently, and whispering softly that another one of her little angels had gone to be with Jesus. I caught my breath and walked over and felt Gena's arm; she was cold, lifeless. Yes, another little angel had died. It was Saturday, October 31, 1901.

Chapter 23

"Ollie, come on in," Mamaw said. "I've been expecting you."

It was Monday, and Gena had been buried that morning. After the funeral service, Mamaw had stopped by the house for only a few minutes. The morning had been cool and breezy, and Mamaw had said she wasn't feeling very well, that she felt like she may be catching cold and was going home to rest. When I walked in, she was sitting in her old rocker in front of the fireplace with her well worn shawl wrapped around her knees, rocking and crying softly.

"How are you feeling, Mamaw?"

"I'll be all right," she replied as she wiped her eyes, "just a little tired and worn out."

I pulled up a chair beside her and sat down. She continued to rock and cry. "I can't believe another baby is dead," she sobbed. "Five precious little ones, gone."

"No, Ma'am," I said. "I can't believe it either."

We sat quietly staring into the fireplace. After a few minutes, Mamaw asked, "How is everything at the house?"

"It's very quiet," I answered. "Not a lot of people have been by. Yesterday afternoon there were only a few of Lizzie's and Papa's friends who came to visit, and this morning there were even fewer. Lizzie's parents and Lottie were the only people who stayed the entire morning. And very few people have brought any food."

Mamaw slowly shook her head and let out a soft sigh. She then took a deep breath and began to cough.

"Are you sure you're okay?" I asked as I leaned over and patted her gently on the back.

"I'll be fine. I got a little chilled at the cemetery, and it gave me a cough. And this crying doesn't help either, but I'll be okay." She then asked, "How is Maude doing?"

"Not very well. She and Octavia came in on the same train from Meridian yesterday afternoon, and I don't know which one was grieving the worst."

"Both of them loved that little girl so much; they were like mothers to her," Mamaw said, "and both so tenderhearted. It hurts to see them so upset."

"When Octavia arrived yesterday, Lizzie put her straight to work fixing cakes and cookies until all hours of the night. Lizzie wanted to make sure there was plenty when people came by today. I think it hurt Octavia's feelings. You know Octavia feels like she is part of the family, and rightly so, and I think she felt like she needed to grieve with us. But last night while she was cooking and crying, I heard her mumble about feeling like hired help, like a slave.

"And Lizzie beats all," I continued, shaking my head. "Not a tear; no sign of grief. Why, this morning she was out of the house early, tending to her *precious* roses, humming to them as if she had no care in the world. She said she was trying to find a late bloom or two, something pretty enough to decorate the kitchen table for all the guests who would be coming. But then this afternoon, she did seem a little upset, not quite her cheery self," I added sarcastically. "My guess is that she was disappointed with the turnout."

"Ollie," my grandmother said sternly, "don't you talk like that. You're being ugly and unkind. Lizzie has been through so much, and speaking like that will not benefit anyone. Five babies! Why, I feel like *I'm* losing the ability to grieve. No family should have to go through what we have been through."

"And Gussie; I can't believe she can be so uncaring," I exclaimed. "Saturday afternoon, the very day that Gena died, she actually asked Papa if it would be okay for her to go to the Halloween carnival at school. She said she didn't see why she should have to sit around the house and do nothing all evening. Papa said no and she has been pouting ever since. Mamaw, that girl can make me so . . . Sometimes I can't believe she is my sister!"

I suddenly realized that anger was getting the best of me. I took a deep breath and let it out slowly, trying to calm myself. Grief and anger are a bad combination. Thoughts that should remain silent are spoken, and actions that are later regretted are taken.

"Mamaw, I'm sorry," I said. "I'm so upset and heartbroken with Gena's death that I can't think straight. Please forgive me for taking my frustrations out on you."

"I understand," Mamaw responded. "It's been a difficult day."

We sat there in silence. It was cool in the house, and after a few minutes, I stood up and walked to the fireplace to warm my hands.

Mamaw softly said, "Tell me about Friday night."

After a moment I turned, and with my back to the fire, I said, "Mamaw it's the strangest thing. Remember when Hugh Lee died . . . has it really been *four* years? I can't believe it's been that long. It seems like yesterday. Remember me telling you about that night? How fitful it was and how I kept having strange dreams? Friday night was the same. I couldn't sleep."

Mamaw interrupted, "With that storm so bad and that horrible thunder and lightening, I don't think anyone in Lauderdale County got much sleep that night."

"Maybe so," I continued, "but when I would doze off, I would have bad dreams, unsettling dreams. Things weren't right. I remember hearing . . . or was I dreaming? . . . Gena was crying, the thunder and lightening had frightened her. Someone got up to comfort her and calm her. And she went back to sleep."

"Could you tell who?" Mamaw asked.

I sat back down and was silent for a moment. "In my dream," I began to choke up, "it was Mama. She was comforting Gena like she would comfort me. Whispering to her the way she would whisper to me."

Mamaw reached over and took my hand. "You still miss her, don't you? I know I do. It's hard to believe she's been gone fifteen years."

"Yes, Ma'am," I answered. "I miss her so much. I often wonder how things would be if Mama was still alive. How different things would probably be."

"Those are questions that can never be answered," Mamaw said. "What might have been."

"I know, Mamaw," I said as I wiped away a few tears.

"Anything else about Friday night?" Mamaw asked.

"Mamaw, for the life of me I can't separate dream from reality. It's all mixed up. Was someone up that night or was it just a dream? Was Gena really crying? Was someone comforting her? I just don't know. I keep running it all through my head but the answer is not there. But Mamaw, a baby doesn't just die. They get sick or they have an accident, but they don't just die. And the fact that Gena should die when Papa and Octavia are gone, it really makes me worry. I feel guilty about having such thoughts, but I can't help it. And then I turn around and think: it doesn't make sense that anyone would want to harm a little baby.

"On top of that, the community response; I don't understand. So few people have been by; so few people came to the funeral. It makes me wonder if the neighbors are also questioning what's going on in our house; wondering why *five* babies have died."

Mamaw let go of my hand and started rocking slowly. "I would be lying if I said I haven't had some of those same thoughts. But as you said, it doesn't make any sense to think that anyone would want to harm our little babies. The only people in the house

Friday night were Lizzie, Gussie, and you. I cannot let myself think that one of you would harm little Gena. And that someone else would sneak into the house to do something like that."

"I agree, it makes no sense," I said. "But I keep wondering are we missing something? Is there a problem that we don't see, or won't let ourselves see? Lizzie? Gussie?"

Mamaw quickly replied, "I can't let myself think that. Lizzie and Gussie have their faults. But evil is not in their hearts. Please don't even suggest that one of them could do such a thing."

We sat silently for a few more minutes.

"Mamaw," I said, "I feel guilty that I couldn't have done something to save Gena."

Mamaw sat quietly and rocked. She was deep in worried thought and I'm not sure she heard me. After another minute I said, "Mamaw, did you notice that Papa buried Gena between Mama and little Stephen? Ever since Mama died, I have somehow been comforted with the thought that when Papa died, I would be able to bury him next to Mama, and they would be side by side forever. But now that will never happen.

"And Mamaw, Papa told me something this morning that I still can't believe. I don't want to believe it. Papa said that Lizzie is pregnant again. She didn't tell him until last night. She's due in May."

Chapter 24

When Gena died Lizzie was about two months along and apparently had suspected it for a few weeks. Why she had not told Papa earlier, I don't know, and why she chose to tell him the night before Gena's funeral is even more perplexing. The news was a surprise, or rather a shock, to the entire family, but it seemed to be especially upsetting to Papa. Papa was a very private man and never voiced his feelings, but that morning when he told me that Lizzie was pregnant, he was obviously upset and said that a new baby is the last thing our family needed right now. And he was right. The next seven months would prove to be very difficult for the entire family.

The family tried to settle back into some sort of normalcy after Gena's funeral, but it never happened. When Dr. Knox learned that Lizzie was pregnant again, he recommended bed rest, as he done with her previous pregnancies. He said that she was in no shape to do anything but rest and let the baby inside her grow. Octavia stayed on as housekeeper and cook. I don't know why I thought she would leave; when Gena died I expected her to pack up and be gone. But she was not one to run away from difficulties. In fact, she took on an even greater role in keeping our home functional.

In the weeks to follow, it became apparent to me that our little town was also having difficulty dealing with Gena's death. The entire community changed in how it related to our family. When we met people in town, the greetings were short and to the point. Conversations were not warm and friendly like they had been. At the depot, business went on as usual, but the inside of the station seemed as cold as the November weather outside. Even at church, where we had always gone to find comfort with our closest, dearest friends, we were greeted politely, but we felt almost like strangers. There was never anything said by anyone, but it was obvious that things had changed.

At first, I was hurt. How could our friends do this to us? Then the hurt turned to anger. There was no reason for us to be treated this way; we had done nothing wrong. But now, as I look back, I can't really blame them. How could people *not* start wondering? I wondered what was going on myself.

Lizzie, confined to the bed, was not exempt from Lockhart's coldness. No one, except her mother, Charlotte, and her sister, Lottie, came to visit. And Lizzie didn't handle it well. She would send Octavia through the neighborhood inviting friends and family over for a visit, but excuses were made. Lizzie became more insistent, sending Octavia out scouring the neighborhood almost every day. Why, it was almost Christmas and people needed entertaining! But soon she became upset and discouraged and gave up sending invitations. She became withdrawn and depressed. And what upset me the most was that she seemed more disturbed over the lack of visitors than the loss of her fifth child.

Just before Christmas 1901, Papa dropped a major bomb shell on our family. Papa and Lizzie decided to leave Lockhart.

Two days before Christmas I stopped by the general store on my way home from the station. It was late afternoon, but already dark on this cool winter day. Papa was going over the receipts for the day, about ready to close up. Everyone else had left.

"Papa, how was business today?" I asked as I tossed my hat on the counter and poured myself a cup of coffee.

"It was fairly busy," Papa answered without looking up. "It's almost Christmas and people are hunting for gifts."

I took a sip of coffee and almost spit it out. "This coffee is terrible. It tastes like tar. This stuff must have been sitting around all day."

"It *is* the end of the day, Ollie," Papa said. "I usually don't brew a fresh pot after one o'clock. But you're welcome to fix yourself a fresh pot."

"No thanks, I'll just wait until we get home," I remarked as I poured out my cup and sat down by the stove. "What I really would like right now is a Coca-Cola. Papa, when are you going to start stocking Coca-Cola? You know they've been bottling it for the past four or five years, and it stays fresh and fizzy for months. I bet you could sell cases of it. Why, the only time I can get it is when I'm in Meridian, and it sure would be nice to enjoy it here."

Papa looked up at me and laughed. "If it's bottled and stays fresh for months, why don't you just buy yourself several bottles the next time you're in Meridian and bring them home with you?"

I remember feeling so dumb. "Papa, that's a great idea. I don't know why I didn't think of that."

Papa finished his paperwork, and placed the receipts in the safe. "Oliver," he said as he turned toward me. "I was planning to talk to you tonight, but since we're alone, I think here would be better."

When he called me Oliver I was either in trouble or he was about to deliver some very important news.

He took a deep breath. "Lizzie and I have decided to move to Meridian. We're planning to leave after the New Year. Lockhart is slowly drying up, and your Uncle John says there is so much opportunity for success in Meridian."

I was speechless. I didn't know what to say. It had never entered my mind to leave Lockhart.

"You're welcome to come with us or, if you wish, you can live here in the house as long as you like. You're twenty-four years old now and can make your own choices. I haven't told Gussie or your Mamaw yet, and I hope they will be understanding. I plan to tell Gussie tonight, and I'll stop by and tell Mother in the morning."

My mind started to race, and I realized there was more to the move than the fact that Lockhart was drying up. It was true that few people were moving in and several families had left, but Papa's general store was successful, and there was no sign of business slowing down. Family and friends were here. Other than Uncle John and Aunt Florence, we knew practically no one in Meridian.

"Papa," I cautiously asked, "there's more to it than what you're telling me, isn't there?"

He walked around the counter and sat down beside me. "Yes, son, there is. You know as well as I do that Lizzie has not been able to cope with Gena's death. For the past two months, her depression has been getting worse and worse, and I don't see things changing for the better. I'm hoping that a move away from the house, away from this town, will help her. I have talked with Dr. Knox, and he agrees that a move would be best for Lizzie."

I knew that there was even more to their decision to move. The coldness of our neighbors and the cloud of suspicion that was beginning to grip our town were obvious. But I decided not to ask any more questions. Gena's death was affecting our family in a frightening way, unlike the deaths of my four brothers.

Chapter 25

"Mamaw, how is Christmas cooking coming along?" I asked. We had closed the depot early due to Christmas Eve, and I was by her house a little earlier than usual.

"Heaven sakes!" Mamaw exclaimed as she almost dropped a bottle of milk. "You almost scared me to death. I wasn't expecting you for another two hours, and I didn't hear you come through the door."

"I'm sorry," I said. "I didn't mean to scare you, Mamaw. Your hearing must be getting bad. The way the front steps creak and this door squeaks, I wouldn't think anyone could sneak up on you. AND DO I NEED TO SPEAK LOUDER, TOO?" I shouted and then laughed.

"Don't make fun of me, young man. Someday you'll see what it's like to get old and deaf." Mamaw grinned. "My eyesight is still good and my right arm is as strong as ever, and you are not too old for a good old-fashioned whipping."

"You know I'm just playing with you, Mamaw," I joked. "This kitchen sure smells good. I can't wait for Christmas dinner. Anything to sample right now?"

"Not yet," she answered. "Octavia is doing most of the cooking for tomorrow, but I told her I would help with the desserts. None of the cakes or pies are quite ready, but if you want some of this apple pie filling, you're welcome to it."

"No thanks, I'll wait, but I may stop by later for a piece of the finished product."

"Has Maude gotten here yet?" Mamaw asked.

"Yes, Ma'am," I answered. "She came in on the last train from Meridian today, but she almost missed it. M & O decided to trim down the schedule for today and tomorrow since it's Christmas Eve, and the last train of the day left Meridian at one o'clock. With all the rain this week, their wagon got stuck in the mud. There were four girls from the school trying to catch that train, and when they realized they were going to be late, they just left their trunks in the wagon and trekked through the mud to the station. The driver said that he would ship the trunks as soon as he could. When the girls finally got to the station, the fireman was working up a steam ready to pull out, but they made it. They were determined not to spend Christmas Eve in Meridian.

"And Maude, what a mess! When she got here, she had mud up to her knees. She's been home now for an hour, and I bet she's still working on those shoes. All those little lace up holes in her new high top shoes; she may never get the mud out. She doesn't have any more shoes with her, and with the limited schedule, her trunk won't get here until tomorrow afternoon. Her Christmas gifts are in her trunk, too, so we won't be opening her gifts until late in the day.

"After the train came through not much was going on at the depot, so I let everyone go early."

"That was nice of you, Ollie. I'm sure everybody appreciated it."

"Oh, by the way," I said, "an interesting wire came across today. Mamaw, do you remember me telling you about wireless telegraph? It's something that's been developing in England for the past few years."

"Yes, I think I remember you saying something about it a while back, but it didn't make any sense to me," she answered.

"Well," I continued, "I've been hearing and reading about it for the past few years. It's really fascinating. There are no wires; the dots and dashes are sent through the air by a transmitter and picked up by a receiver. They've been doing a lot of work with it in England. They have actually been able to transmit from one island to another. A week and a half ago, on December 12, a signal was sent across the Atlantic Ocean for the first time, from a place in Ireland to Signal Hill in St. John's, Newfoundland. An Italian named Guglielmo Marconi did it. He used a kite with a four-hundred-foot line hooked to the receiver in order to get the message, and it worked. The message was 'dot.dot.dot,' which is Morse code for 'S.'"

"Four hundred foot line?" she asked with a confused look on her face. "Why, that could never reach Ireland. It's got to be a thousand miles away."

"No, Mamaw," I said shaking my head. "The wire was straight up in the air, connected to a kite, so that the signal from Ireland could be received."

"Well, that doesn't make any sense to me," Mamaw said as she turned back to her cooking. "And besides, that Italian man, Ugly Elmo, what a name! Who does he think he is, Benjamin Franklin?" She began to laugh at her own little joke.

I decided it was a lost cause to get my grandmother to understand this truly amazing new occurrence.

"Ollie," Mamaw said in a more serious tone. "Your Papa came by this morning. He told me they're going to move to Meridian after Christmas. He said that he and Lizzie have been talking about it for the past two weeks and made the decision last night."

"Yes, Ma'am, that's the decision they have made."

"What are you going to do? Are you going with them or staying here?" she asked.

"I haven't made up my mind yet. I've got to think about it for a while. What about you?"

"It's hard to believe," Mamaw answered, "but I've been back in Lockhart now for over fifteen years. Sometimes it seems like such a short time and other times it seems like forever. I've been fortunate to have made a lot of good friends here, especially Lizzie's parents, T. W. and Charlotte, but I've still got a lot of friends in Meridian. I've been thinking all morning, and I've decided to go back to Meridian. Your Papa said that I would be welcome to live with them. He said it was time to leave, and I think he is right.

"This town has changed since Gena died. Lizzie is miserable. She says she doesn't have a friend in town; all she does is lie in bed and cry. And I've felt a coldness from the people over the past two months that chills me to the bone and it upsets me so much. I can't believe they are treating us this way."

"I feel it too, Mamaw. But I don't think people are doing it on purpose. Our family's tragedies have affected them, too. They are confused and worried, and like me, they can't find a peace about it. I think they find being around us awkward and uncomfortable; they don't know what to say or do. So they try to ignore us and it comes across as being rude and cold."

"Maybe so," Mamaw said, "but I don't like it and I can't live like this. Hopefully people in Meridian will treat us better."

"I'm sure they will. They haven't been touched with all our losses," I replied.

"Octavia is happy about the return to Meridian," I continued, "but Gussie is fit to be tied. At seventeen and in her last year of school, she wants no part in starting all over. More important, she's got a beau. Need Jarman has been courting her and she doesn't want to be ten miles away from him. It would be a long two-and-a-half-hour buggy ride or a fairly expensive trip by train away from him, and I don't think she can stand it."

"I understand your Papa's not happy about him," Mamaw said.

"Papa said he wouldn't give a 'V' nickel for Need, and I agree. I've known him all my life. He's not dependable and I doubt he will ever amount to anything. I think Papa sees the move as a chance to get Gussie away from him."

Mamaw shook her head. "Gussie's been sweet on him for several months, and as hard-headed as she is, she won't let a little distance cool things off."

I watched Mamaw as she rolled out a soft pie crust and gently pressed it into one of her pie tins. She trimmed off the excess with a knife and poured the filling out of the bowl into the crust. She then used a wooden spoon to spread the filling out evenly. I couldn't stand it, so I reached into the bowl with two fingers and got a bite of sweet, warm, delicious apple pie filling.

"I thought you were going to wait for the final product."

"I couldn't wait," I said, as I licked my fingers clean. "It looked too good to pass up. I just had to have some now."

Mamaw paused for a moment and shook her head. "I'm afraid that's what Gussie and Need are saying to each other, too. 'Just can't wait. Have to have a taste now.' I worry about her. But you know as well as I do that you can't tell her anything. She's stubborn as a mule and does what she wants. I sure hope she doesn't do anything rash and get her self in trouble."

I was stunned by her frankness about Gussie and Need. It was a concern that I hadn't really thought about. In fact I didn't *want* to think about it. So I acted like I didn't hear her.

"Papa's heading to Meridian after the first of the year to find a house and to talk with Uncle John about work. Papa thinks he can still keep his businesses going here in Lockhart and may be able to start some new ones in Meridian." (And he did. Being a good, honest businessman, his new endeavors in Meridian were more than successful. Over the next twenty-five years, as people began to leave Lockhart and as Meridian continued to grow, the move to Meridian would be seen as a wise business decision.) "With Lizzie due in May, he wants to be all moved in by the middle of February."

I paused for a moment and then said, "Mamaw, tell me what you think about Lizzie and the move and about her and this baby she's going to have."

Mamaw finished putting a layer of pie crust over the filling and placed it in the oven. She then sat down beside me. "I don't know," she said. "I really don't know what to expect. Lizzie has changed so much over the past few years. Sorrow and tragedy have been so unkind to her. She's just not the same person she was when your Papa asked her to marry him. And she's not the same mother she was when little Stephen and Timothy were here. But I'm hoping that the move, a new home, new friends, and new surroundings will give her a new start, make her more like she used to be. You know that at one time she *was* a loving mother, and I hope she can be one again. But I do worry about her."

"Do you worry about this child?" I asked cautiously.

"No, Ollie. I can't let myself think such thoughts."

Chapter 26

My decision to leave Lockhart was difficult. Our home was the only home I had ever known. I had never spent any time away from our tiny community. Except for the nights I slept under the stars as a youth, I can count on one hand the number of nights I had been away from home, and all of those at Uncle John's home in Meridian. My only friends were in Lockhart.

But I decided to move. I based my decision to move on three things. First, Meridian was booming and Lockhart was stagnant. In the past ten years very few families had moved to Lockhart. Lockhart was a farming community, and most of the young people with ambitions beyond the farm were heading to Meridian after completing school. (In the coming years when automobiles and better roads would make travel to Meridian a quick and easy excursion, all work, except farming, would disappear from Lockhart.)

Secondly, there was family. I don't think I could have been happy in Lockhart without the companionship and love of my family. Papa was a wonderful father and friend, and in spite of their problems, Lizzie and Gussie were still family. And then there was Mamaw; my confidant, my encourager, and my best friend. If she had stayed in Lockhart, I would have stayed. I had a feeling that if I had asked her to stay, she would have, but deep down, like everyone, except Gussie, I was ready to go.

Thirdly, I had no prospects of getting married. I was twenty-four years old and not getting any younger. In a small community, the number of potential brides is limited, and all the members of the fairer sex in Lockhart were either married or single for a reason. Meridian was a town of 25,000 and hopefully would afford a better selection. (I found me a bride, but it took six years.) And as for living arrangements, as long as I was unmarried I would live with Papa and Lizzie.

Papa's trip to Meridian after Christmas was a success. He found and purchased a house on the south side on 25th Street, less than two blocks from Hawkins Memorial Church. In February 1902, we started the slow move from Lockhart to Meridian.

There were no big good-byes and no parties with friends telling us how they hated to see us go. However, a few of Papa and Lizzie's closest friends did stop by to wish us well. My coworkers at the station were kind enough to tell me how much they had enjoyed working with me and how they hoped things would go well for us. T. W. and Charlotte, Lizzie's parents, were the only people who seemed genuinely saddened that we were leaving. Charlotte cried the entire time that we were packing, but between sobs, said that she understood: that the move was for the best. Our minister at the Methodist church, Reverend Lewis, came by as we were packing. He offered up a prayer that we would have a safe move and that we would find happiness and peace in our new home.

The move went well but took several days and several trips. Our wagon could hold just so much. Papa and I furnished most of the labor, but he hired a couple of colored men to help with the heavy stuff. Octavia was the sergeant, directing what furniture went where, making sure nothing would get broken or scratched. Gussie grudgingly helped pack dishes, kitchenware, and clothes in crates. Lizzie, great with child, obeyed Dr. Knox's insistence to rest and only observed. Papa decided to transport Maude's piano by train. As with its move from Meridian, its move back to Meridian by wagon would have been a noisy disaster. Lizzie was also transported by train, along with the piano, on the ten-mile trip.

The one thing that Lizzie hated to leave behind in Lockhart was her roses. For over ten years she had nurtured and pampered those bushes, and she hated that she couldn't just dig them up and take every one of them to Meridian. Papa said that it would probably be easier to get some fresh cuttings from the original bush and start over and in no time she would have them blooming.

The house that Papa bought was huge. It was an attractive, well built two-story white wood structure with six bedrooms, a large living area, and separate parlor and dining areas. To Octavia's delight, the kitchen was roomy. Instead of the cast iron wood burning stove we had in Lockhart, there was a natural gas stove with three burners and a double oven. She was in heaven. (And I didn't miss keeping the wood bin filled either.)

Another big change was the presence of gas heaters. In Lockhart, we relied on fireplaces and the stove to ward off the cold, but in our new home we had gas heaters located throughout the house that kept us nice and comfortable through the cold winter nights. (Electricity was just beginning to reach our part of the country and it would be a few years before our house would be wired.)

There were four bedrooms upstairs and two downstairs. Papa and Lizzie had one of the first floor rooms, and Mamaw, with her bad knees and hips, claimed the other. Octavia, Gussie, and I were upstairs, and Maude, seeing an empty room, decided to move in. For the past two years Maude had been living in a boarding house with eight other girls, two to a room, so she jumped at the chance to come home to a private room. Papa didn't mind; unlike the boarding house, the room upstairs was free.

Living in Meridian proved to be much different than living in Lockhart. Lockhart had only about a hundred residents living in twenty-five homes; it was a quiet, peaceful hamlet with forests and fields spreading out from the houses in every direction. Meridian, with 25,000, was a busy metropolis. There were people everywhere; instead of fields and forests, there were houses and more houses.

Since I had spent a fair amount of time in Meridian over the past few years on business with the M & O, I knew my way around the city fairly well. But living there was quite different. I was not uncomfortable with the town and crowds, but I had always been able to retreat to Lockhart and its slow, peaceful pace. Now I was only able to retreat into my home. (Meridian would one day seem like such a quaint little town, when a few years later I would move to Dallas, Texas.)

As far as work was concerned, I did quite well in the move. Good telegraphers were hard to find, and the M & O Railroad had no problems with transferring me to the busier Meridian depot. Even though it was a demotion in title from depot manager to telegrapher, the pay was actually better and the work harder. Lockhart had been a quiet, slow little station, and Meridian was anything but quiet. The wire at the Meridian depot was continually humming, and I was kept plenty busy with my beloved "dots and dashes." And with free room and board, I was able to build up a nice little nest egg for the future.

The move was also very successful for Papa. As he had hoped, he was able to continue the farm supply store and general store in Lockhart. Two or three times each month he would catch the early morning train to Lockhart, check on his stores, and be back in Meridian by dark.

In Meridian, Papa's entrepreneurial skills led to even greater success. His first endeavor was another general store, which he built next door to our home on 25th Avenue. Soon he was making a respectable return on that investment and he used that success to breed even more success.[1]

Papa and Uncle John purchased the railroad spur connecting Meridian to Union, Mississippi. Union, thirty miles northwest of Meridian, had become a primary switching station for the Alabama and Vicksburg Railway, and had developed into a thriving little community. The thirty-mile passenger route from Meridian to Union was soon nicknamed the "Doodle Bug" line.

Papa also purchased a tract of land in downtown Union, a half block from the railroad station, and built a three-story hotel. The Hotel Parker became the center of activity in this small town for many years. The hotel restaurant became famous throughout the region for its delicious food, served family style.

The Hotel Parker was sold in 1923 to a family by the name of Sessums. Today, in 1952, the Sessums Hotel and Restaurant continues to be a thriving business run by Ma Sessums, who carries on the tradition of the wonderful home style meals.[2]

Papa also was able to find enough spare time to become a part time conductor on the A & V Railroad, working the Meridian to Union route, which made it very convenient for him to check on his Union investment.

Chapter 27

In April 1902, a few weeks after moving to Meridian, as we seemed to be settling in and getting acquainted with our new town, Gussie disappeared. She had been unhappy with the move, and she let us know it. All she did was pout and cry about how she missed her friends back in Lockhart. Papa told her that once she got into school she would find some new friends and everything would be fine.

School! Well, as far as Gussie was concerned, the idea of enrolling in school was out of the question. Why, there was no reason on earth that she would want to go to school with a bunch of "citified" strangers! But Papa intervened. With only four months of school remaining and a diploma waiting, he "encouraged" her to enroll, which she did reluctantly.

It was Sunday morning and everyone except Gussie was up enjoying a leisurely breakfast before heading down the street to church. Octavia was shaking her head, saying that Gussie was going to be late if she didn't hurry up. She yelled up the stairwell several times for Gussie to get herself downstairs, but there was no response. After a few minutes Octavia headed up the stairs, shaking her head and mumbling something about "lazy spoiled white girls." She opened the bedroom door, and to her surprise, Gussie was not there. There was no note, no hint at all, except that most of her clothes were also gone.

It was two weeks before we heard anything from Gussie, but we were able to put two and two together. Sunday afternoon I headed down to the depot and sent a wire to Lockhart to inquire about Need Jarman. Several hours later a wire returned stating that his parents couldn't find him and asked if we knew where he was. Papa was fit to be tied. I think that if he could have found them, he would have strangled them both. But there was nothing we could do. We had nowhere to start and no leads; we just had to wait.

Two weeks later Need and Gussie showed up in Lockhart, a married couple, and their story unfolded. Need's family said that he had been moping around for several weeks since Gussie had left Lockhart. On the Saturday of their "elopement" he said something about how he couldn't take it any longer, and then disappeared. That afternoon he made it to Meridian on foot and hid behind our back fence until he could get Gussie's attention.

They planned for her to sneak out of the house during the night, and the two of them would catch the M &O train south to New Augusta, ninety miles away. They would get married, and start a life there. Steps one and two of their plan occurred, but step three fell through. They made it to New Augusta and got married, but things didn't fall into place like they thought it would.

Need had little money and after two weeks of looking for a job, the purse was almost empty, and he got discouraged. Like the prodigal son, but with a bride by his side, he realized that they would be better off in Lockhart where at least they could depend on his parents for food and a roof over their heads.

They had just enough money to buy two train tickets back to Meridian. When they arrived, they decided not to stop by and see us, but headed on to Lockhart. I think Need was worried about there being a shotgun, but in reality, Papa's feelings were hurt that they totally bypassed us.

Need and Gussie moved into Mamaw's old cottage in Lockhart. Papa had been unable to sell it and was more than generous in letting them stay there for free for as long as they wished. Need found steady work at a sawmill north of town. The pay was not much, but he was able to put food on the table.

On May 18, 1902, another happy, healthy little girl, Elizabeth Parker was born. Soon it became obvious that she had *four* mothers: Lizzie who birthed her and provided the milk, Mamaw, Maude, and Octavia who provided the love and nurture. It also became apparent that very little love would flow from Lizzie to this new arrival. She fed her willingly and met her needs, but handled her in a cold "stand-offish" manner. There was no mistreatment, just indifference. Apparently, the move to Meridian had not changed Lizzie.

In July 1902, Lizzie's father, T. W. Bludworth, died in Lockhart. Lizzie's mother, Charlotte, said that he had gone to the cornfield early that morning. When he hadn't returned by midmorning, she went to check on him and found him under an oak tree, slumped over, dead of an apparent heart attack. At the funeral we visited with several of our old neighbors and friends, who asked how we were doing in Meridian. They politely said that they missed us, but as when we had left five months ago, they seemed rather distant.

Lizzie took her father's death very hard. For the next several days she did not come out of her room and her depression seemed worse. I wanted to ask her, "Why could you not have mourned like this for Hugh Lee, and Roger, and Gena? T. W. was your father, but these were your beautiful little babies whose lives ended so early."

As Elizabeth grew, my concern for her grew as well. I would lie awake at night thinking about her. And each day as I looked at her I would wonder, what is your future? Will you grow to be a young lady? Will you be a wife and mother? Will you know the love of grandchildren? Will you feel the aches and pains of old age? Or will you join five little Angels in Lockhart Cemetery?

Until Gena died, there was never a question in my mind about the deaths of my siblings. Little Stephen died of whooping cough, Timothy of typhoid fever. Roger died of what appeared to be accidental scalding. Hugh Lee's death was unexplainable, but I thought one in four, there was no pattern. But with Gena's death being unexplained, I began to wonder. I finally got up the courage to speak to my father about my concern.

One Saturday afternoon in August 1902, Papa and I were sitting on the front porch. All the ladies, including Octavia, had gone into town to do some shopping, and we were left with the responsibility of babysitting three month old Elizabeth. She was asleep inside and we were enjoying a little quiet time. It was hot and humid, a day when one didn't want to do anything but sit and fan. We talked about work, the weather, and how we couldn't wait 'til the cool winds of fall arrived; we wondered about Need and Gussie and how they were doing in Lockhart.

"It's hard to believe," Papa said. "It's been six months since we moved from Lockhart. It seems like only yesterday when we were loading up the wagon and making all those trips to get everything moved. I found things squirreled away in that old house that I had forgotten I ever had." He smiled and continued, "Ollie, I bought that house a week after I married your Mama, almost twenty-five years ago."

After a few moments of silence, I asked, "Papa, what do you think about the move? Do you think it was the right thing for the family and for Lizzie?"

Papa thought for a moment and then replied, "I feel good about it. It was the right thing to do. But I do worry about Lizzie.

She had been through so much, and it's going to take her a while to recover. Elizabeth is only three months old and Lizzie is just now getting out of the house. I hope that as she makes friends and gets used to the town, her happiness will return."

I took a deep breath and asked, "Papa, do you have any concerns about the deaths of any of the babies or any concerns about Elizabeth?"

He slowly stood up and walked over to the porch railing. He stood there for a moment, then turned around, and looked me straight in the eye. "No, Ollie, I don't," he said with a hint of anger in his voice. "I'm aware of all the rumors going around in Lockhart. I'm not blind or deaf. But I cannot allow myself to think that those deaths were anything but God's will."

He choked up at this point and said, "The deaths of those babies have just about destroyed my wife." He paused, trying to gather himself, and then continued, "You know, people sometimes forget about how tragedy affects the other parent, the father; those deaths have torn my heart apart, too. I've been able to handle it better than Lizzie, but at times I just feel like giving up. And, no, Ollie, I'm not worried about Elizabeth; I can't let myself worry about her. If I did, it would drive me crazy. I trust my wife and my family."

From inside the house we heard a little whimper. Elizabeth was waking up. Papa smiled and then walked into the house. A few moments later he was back outside with Elizabeth in his arms, telling her how much he loved his little daughter. Papa looked old, older than I had ever realized. In just the few moments it had taken him to get Elizabeth, he seemed to have become an old man, like an aged grandfather, stooped and worn out. But then, he was almost fifty years old.

I wish that I could say that my conversation with Papa lifted my fears and doubts, but it didn't. I continued to worry but felt there wasn't anything else to do. I had to leave the future in God's hand and pray that my fears were unfounded.

Chapter 28

Elizabeth grew to be a happy, healthy little girl, and with all the attention of Octavia, Maude, and Mamaw, she was also spoiled. I don't think she knew what the floor was because she was always in somebody's lap.

The winter months passed and spring arrived early. This particular winter was rather mild and we didn't have a single freeze that year. There may have been a frost once or twice, but no really cold weather. By the end of February, the trees were beginning to bud and the daffodils began to raise their little yellow heads. Life was quiet.

Papa and I had settled into our new working conditions. Mamaw and Octavia were sharing the household duties and looking after Elizabeth. Maude was in her third year of college and doing exceptionally well in her music studies. Gussie and Need, whom we rarely saw, were just scraping by in Lockhart.

And then there was Lizzie. With the early spring her white roses took root and began to sprout new growth. And not only did her flowers flourish, Lizzie seemed to blossom forth, too. It had been a year since we had moved from Lockhart, and the family had pretty much accepted the fact that the withdrawn sadness that Lizzie had brought to Meridian would never go away. But it seemed like overnight the sadness disappeared and happiness returned. Soon Lizzie was getting out and meeting the neighbors and inviting them over for tea and cookies (provided by Octavia). She even inquired about all of the ladies' organizations in town and joined one. She was soon thriving on Meridian's social scene.

One of Lizzie's endeavors that I became particularly fond of was the Grand Opera House. "The Lady," as it was affectionately known, was a beautiful Victorian opera house which opened downtown in 1890. It was a huge building and would seat over a thousand people. When I walked in for the first time, I couldn't believe the beauty! I had never been in a building that size in my life. There were massive dark red curtains that were raised and lowered for the performances. Red carpet covered the floor. There were a thousand fancy cloth-covered chairs that folded up behind you when you stood up, and gas lamps which illuminated the entire room.

It was said that "The Lady" rivaled the opera houses in New Orleans and Atlanta, and she attracted many of the best performers in the world to our little city. Papa, Lizzie, Maude, and I enjoyed many a night of entertainment featuring opera greats like Madame Gadski and Madame Sherry. I especially liked the traveling entertainment shows, called vaudeville acts, which came through every few weeks and played to sold out crowds. Mamaw never would go; said she had no interest in hearing fat ladies singing at the top of their lungs. Octavia never went either. There was a section for the colored folk in the balcony, and I offered to pay her way, but each time she declined, saying she wanted to stay home and keep Mamaw company.

The Grand Opera house entertained the citizens of Meridian for over thirty years with some of the finest entertainment found in the world. In 1923, as vaudeville disappeared and moving pictures appeared, "The Lady" was leased to Saenger Films of New Orleans and was converted to a movie house. In 1928, her doors were closed and have remained closed to this day.[3]

Although Lizzie's social life bloomed, her affection for Elizabeth did not. She continued to have that distant, detached relationship which seemed unchanged from the first day Elizabeth entered this world. But that changed abruptly in late March 1903.

Late one afternoon I came home from the depot, and Lizzie and Mamaw were sitting on the porch. Mamaw was rocking in her favorite old rocker that we had brought from Lockhart, and Lizzie was sitting quietly in the swing holding little Elizabeth, now almost eleven months old.

As I approached the porch, I heard Mamaw say, "The baby looks fine to me. She doesn't look sick at all."

Lizzie had a concerned look on her face and looked at me. "Ollie, do you think Elizabeth looks well? For the past few days, she's looked a little ill to me. I'm worried that she's getting sick."

I reached down and took Elizabeth in my arms, looked her over as well as a bachelor could, and couldn't see anything wrong. She seemed happy and playful, without any cough, cold, or runny nose. She didn't feel warm or flushed.

"Lizzie, I agree with Mamaw, I think she's just fine."

Lizzie shook her head and said, "I'm still concerned. She just doesn't look right to me."

For the next few days Lizzie continued to be concerned about Elizabeth's health. She would look at her closely and declare there was something wrong with her. Yet, we could see nothing wrong. Elizabeth was as healthy and happy as I had ever seen her. After several days, Papa said that even though he didn't think anything was wrong, he would send for the doctor and let him check her out if it would make Lizzie feel better.

Having been in Meridian for only a year, we had not used the services of a doctor and didn't know one. When Lizzie delivered Elizabeth eleven months before, there was no doctor in attendance. She said that she had birthed five babies without any problems and didn't need a doctor she didn't know holding her hand. A neighbor recommended that we use a Dr. Tatum, and I was elected to find his office and ask him to come and check out our little Elizabeth.

Dr. Tatum was fairly young, not much older than I was, and had recently opened his practice in Meridian. I suspect that he, like most young physicians just starting out, was spending a fair amount of time staring at the ceiling, hoping that his practice would grow. He was more than happy to make a house call to check on Elizabeth.

When Dr. Tatum arrived he sat little Elizabeth in his lap, inspected her tiny fingernails and toenails, looked at the whites of her eyes, and struggled to look in her ears, nose, and mouth as she squirmed in his lap. He thumped on her little chest and abdomen, listened to her heart and lungs with his stethoscope, and felt her neck for lumps and bumps. After ten minutes, he proudly proclaimed that he had never seen such a healthy specimen. We thanked him and he bid us good-bye.

Lizzie was not satisfied. "That young doctor looks wet behind the ears," she said. "He's obviously too inexperienced to know what he's doing. I sure wish that old Dr. Knox in Lockhart could take a look at her."

"I really don't see any need in making a trip to Lockhart," Papa responded, "but if in a few days you are still concerned, we will go. Besides," he added, "it will be a good excuse to visit with Gussie and Need, and to see how your mother is doing. It's hard to believe that it's been almost nine months since T. W. died."

I don't think it would have made any difference, but for Papa's sake, I wish that we had gone to see Dr. Knox that very moment.

Two days later, April 1, 1903, started out as any day. Octavia cooked a breakfast of pancakes, scrambled eggs, and bacon. Papa and I headed to work and Maude went to school. Mamaw and Oc-tavia headed to the market to check out the spring vegetables. Mamaw was hoping to find some fresh turnip greens and carrots, and with the early spring, maybe even some strawberries. She said it was a shame that we no longer had our own garden and had to rely on a market for such basic food. Lizzie wasn't feeling well so she stayed home with the baby.

My morning at the station was not unusually busy, with a fair amount of activity on the wire: messages to be sent and received. At about eleven, I was deep in thought as I was tapping out a fairly long wire, when I looked up to see Octavia standing in front of my desk. She was out of breath. She was holding a handkerchief over her mouth and sobbing softly.

"Mister Ollie," she said, "you need to come home. Elizabeth is dead."

Chapter 29

"Mamaw, let's stay here for a while longer. I'll tell Papa to head on back to Meridian in the wagon with Lizzie, Maude, and Octavia, and we'll follow along later in the buggy."

The burial had been quiet. Only a few of Papa's and Lizzie's closest Lockhart friends had attended. In fact, there were more friends and neighbors who came from Meridian than from Lockhart. Reverend Lewis, Lockhart Methodist Church's long-time minister, had been ill for the past several weeks and was unable to perform the service. Our minister at Hawkins Memorial was kind to make the trip to preside over the sad event.

Mamaw and I sat down on the church steps as the two colored men filled in the tiny grave. Mamaw had been on her feet most of the day, and her arthritic knees needed a rest.

We sat quietly for a while, and then Mamaw said, "It was good to see Charlotte today. She seems to have adjusted fairly well to life without T. W. She's fortunate to have those two boys, Junius and James, close by to help with chores. Her health is still good, but there is only so much around a farm that a woman can do. I have really missed visiting with her since we have moved. She had become one of my closest friends."

"Yes, Ma'am," I replied, "she has done well, and the farm doesn't seem to have suffered at all."

"I don't see how those two boys have been able to keep things going," Mamaw added, "since both of them have jobs of their own. That farm is a full time job by itself."

"Junius is finding that out," I said. "He's about to quit his job at the sawmill and devote all his time to the farm. He said he can't do both. He also said that James is talking about moving to Jackson to find work. You know he has never liked farm work and almost everything else in this little town has just about dried up."

"I don't blame him," Mamaw said. "This town seems to be slowly dying. No new life coming in, and a lot of families leaving. And talking about the sawmill, did Junius have anything to say about how Need is working out?"

"He said he's pretty worthless," I replied. "He's always trying to find ways to get out of work. In fact, Junius said that a few days ago he found Need asleep behind a stack of lumber in the middle of the morning. He told him that he was lucky it was he and not the foreman who found him. Otherwise, he would be hunting for another job. But it didn't seem to phase Need at all."

"That's a shame," Mamaw said. "Gussie sure has her hands full with him. I should feel sorry for her, but as the saying goes, 'she made her own bed; now she has to lie in it.' What in the world will those two do when a baby comes along? And my poor little house! We had it looking so nice and pretty. But now it's such a mess; I don't think Gussie has swept the floor a single time since she moved in. And dirty clothes everywhere. She and Need would rather wear dirty clothes than spend the time washing and cleaning. I wouldn't let the chickens live in that house now."

Soon one of the colored men who had dug the grave walked up and said that the dirt work was finished and we could go back and visit if we wished. Mamaw and I slowly walked back to the cemetery. Everyone else had already left. Papa and the rest of the family and friends from Meridian had already headed back to the big city; the Lockhart few back to their homes. Only Mamaw and I were left.

I looked at the row of eight graves, and thought my heart would break—my little sister, Cornelia, who I barely remembered; my mother who I will always remember; and six half-sisters and brothers: Elizabeth, Gena, Stephen, Timothy, Hugh Lee, and Roger. With those thoughts of sadness, a wave of guilt hit me and made me sick to my stomach. How could this happen? How could these little ones die and I just stand by and do nothing? Was there anything that I could have done? Or was I just stirring up thoughts that had no basis?

As I stood there I suddenly realized that my thoughts were being spoken aloud; but the voice was not mine. It was the voice of my grandmother.

"I just don't understand," Mamaw said. "How could we have let this happen?" She then started crying softly. "Those sweet little babies. I feel so guilty. I would give my life many times over . . . "

It was my turn to comfort and console now. "Mamaw," I said, "there is nothing you could have done."

There was a stone bench next to the family plot and we sat down. After a moment I said, "Mamaw, tell me again what happened the day Elizabeth died. I still don't understand what happened when you and Octavia got home."

"That morning," Mamaw began, "Octavia and I headed to the market shortly after you and Papa left for work. Lizzie stayed home with the baby; she said she wasn't feeling well. She also said she was still worried about Elizabeth and didn't want to take her out. We were at the market for about two hours, bought what we needed, and headed home. It was a beautiful day, not a cloud in the sky. There was a light cool breeze in the air; the perfect spring day to be outside.

"We took our time going home. Octavia walked me down the street where her 'father' had lived. She said she had never been inside, nor had she ever had a real conversation with him. She had spoken to him only a few times, and then it had been just a polite 'how do you do, sir.' She said she used to dream that she would run up to the front door of his big house. There he would be standing in the doorway with a big smile on his face, and he would sweep her up in his arms. He would take her inside, and she would play for hours with her little white brothers and sisters. It almost made me cry listening to her talk about the father and the family she wished she had.

"We then headed home," she continued. "When we got to the house, it was quiet, but we really didn't think anything about it. Lizzie wasn't feeling well and was probably resting, and it was nap time for Elizabeth. Octavia and I headed to the kitchen and started washing the vegetables and preparing for lunch. After a few minutes, Octavia said that she would finish up, so I decided to go check on Lizzie.

"As I dried my hands, I walked into the parlor, and was surprised to see Lizzie lying on the couch, awake, staring at the ceiling. I jumped back, startled, and told her that she almost gave me a heart attack. I then asked how she was feeling. She slowly looked over at me, like she was in another world and said she was feeling okay. I then asked about Elizabeth. After a moment Lizzie turned her head, stared at the ceiling again, took a deep breath, and said that the baby was doing fine. Suddenly a horrible shiver came over me. I dropped the dish towel and ran into the bedroom. The baby was in the crib and the room looked as normal as could be. I let out a sigh of relief, not realizing that I was holding my breath. I laughed to myself, feeling a little silly at the horrible thoughts I was having.

"After I gathered my thoughts, I walked quietly over to the crib to cover Elizabeth. It was a rather cool day. When I touched her little leg, I jumped and let out a scream. She was as cold as ice. Octavia rushed in and I remember crying out that the baby was dead. Octavia picked up little Elizabeth held her close and screamed, 'No, no, not again! Oh, no, Elizabeth, not Elizabeth!' I felt lightheaded, and everything after that is just a blur.

"The next I knew I was sitting on the side of the bed, sobbing. I remember Octavia was standing there, slowly rocking the still, sweet baby, and crying, 'Poor little baby! Oh, poor little baby.' Lizzie was standing beside her, with a ghost-like expression on her face, shaking her head, saying that she had *told* us the baby was ill and nobody would listen. She said it was our fault and Papa's fault for not doing something, and now another one of her angels was dead, gone to be with Jesus. After a few minutes Octavia gently put Elizabeth back in her crib and went to get you and Papa."

"Could you tell if there was anything visibly wrong with Elizabeth?" I asked.

"No," she answered. "No one was able to find anything wrong with her. No rash, no marks on her body. Even Dr. Tatum came and looked her over. He looked in her mouth and throat, wondering if she could have strangled on something, but he found nothing. That young doctor was so upset. Having just examined her two days earlier and now for her to be dead. He couldn't understand it; he just kept shaking his head."

After a few moments, I took a deep breath. "Mamaw," I said cautiously, "do you really think that Elizabeth just *died?*"

"If you're asking me if Lizzie killed this baby, I honestly don't know," she answered bluntly. "I just don't know. Ollie, my mind keeps going over and over that day, trying to remember how Lizzie reacted. And it seems so strange. She acted so detached, like she was somewhere else, looking in. She never cried, she never asked to hold Elizabeth. She just kept telling us it was our fault, that we were to blame. But I can't make myself believe that she killed her baby."

"Mamaw, I have been worrying about something like this happening ever since Elizabeth was born. I even talked with Papa about it a few months ago and he brushed it off. Said the same thing you said. He couldn't, or rather wouldn't, let himself think such thoughts. And now, I feel so guilty. Should I have done something? Could I have done something?"

"Ollie, what would you have done?" Mamaw asked. "What could we have done? The more I think about it, the more I feel there is nothing we could have done. First off, there is no proof that Lizzie did anything to the baby. I will not confront her with such an accusation, and I don't think you can either.

"But suppose she was confronted and confessed to killing Elizabeth, or any of the other babies, what would we do? Call the sheriff? Put her in jail? Put her in a lunatic asylum? That would accomplish nothing. Secondly, what would you have had your father do when you approached him last summer? Take Elizabeth away from her mother just because you were worried? Would you have taken her away yourself? No. As harsh as it seems and as tragic as things have turned out, I don't think that anything could have been done differently. Thirdly, little Elizabeth is dead. We can't change that, and nothing will ever bring her back. I just hope and pray that there will be no more babies. Lizzie is thirty-five; your father is almost fifty."

Mamaw was right. At that point in time, as we looked at the tiny mound of dirt, there was nothing we could do except pray with all our souls that there would never be another angel born to Lizzie Parker.

We sat in silence. I remember thinking how beautiful that April day was; there was a cool breeze and not a cloud in the sky. The dogwood trees were blooming and the grass was a soft, bright green. This should have been a day of celebrating life, not mourning death.

After a few minutes I said, "Mamaw, I think it's time for us to go. It will be dark when we get back to Meridian."

We stood up and walked back over to the little grave. There were fresh picked wildflowers that had been placed at the head of Elizabeth's grave. Mamaw reached down, picked them up, and gently placed them on the mound of dirt that covered little Elizabeth. She then looked down the row of tiny markers and said, "Ollie, there's no more room. No one else should die."

How I wish that she had been right.

The days that followed Elizabeth's funeral were different than the ones following Gena's death in Lockhart. Our new neighbors and friends in Meridian were there to comfort and console. The tables were once more covered with dishes of love and sympathy. People visited by the dozens, telling us how deeply saddened they were at our loss. Lizzie was the hostess, and the world was her guest.

Chapter 30

Again life went on. The world continued to spin, the sun continued to shine, the stars continued to sparkle. For the next several years we settled into living, but there was always a shadow, a pall, that lingered. I continued my work at the depot and drowned myself in my "dots and dashes." Papa spent more and more time with his businesses, which were very successful, but very time-consuming.

Maude finished college, and with no beau in sight, immersed herself in her music. She let it be known throughout the neighborhood that she wanted to teach piano, and before long, had more pupils than she knew what to do with. She also replaced the ageing pianist, Miss Vawter, at Hawkins Memorial Methodist Church, and was soon playing for every function at the church, from weddings, to funerals, to weekly choir practices. (The family had resigned itself to the fact that Maude would be an old maid, until several years later, to everyone's delight, her knight in shining armor finally appeared. In 1910, she married Arthur Simpson Coburn, Sr., and over the next eight years bore him three sons and a daughter.)

Octavia ran the household, kept us all in line, and was becoming more a part of the family with each passing day.

Mamaw continued to age, and her arthritis was taking a toll on her health. That is, until a miracle drug appeared: Aspirin—acetylsalicylic acid. In 1897, Felix Hoffman, a research assistant for Friedrick Bayer and Company of Germany, synthesized this white powder pain killer, and on March 6, 1899, it was patented. (Felix also developed heroin that same year.) Bayer Aspirin would become a miracle cure, the preferred non-narcotic painkiller for decades to come. When it finally reached the Deep South a few years later, Mamaw's unwelcome companion, "Arthur Itis," was sent packing, and she felt like dancing! Maybe not dancing, but aspirin did make her last several years pain-free and more enjoyable.

Over the next few years, Lizzie's social life continued to blossom. She became involved in every society event possible; her only limiting factor was that there were only twenty-four hours in a day. With Papa's success in business, there was money to allow her to look and act the part of a "turn-of-the-century" socialite. She never talked about babies, never reminisced about the past, never seemed to have sad memories. I could not comprehend how she could dismiss the past so easily. Otherwise, she seemed as normal, well-adjusted, and happy as any other woman in Meridian, living in the here and now, thriving on entertaining and being entertained.

When she was not off with her social activities, she was usually in her rose garden. The new cuttings responded to her pampering and pruning, and before long her bushes were as full and beautiful as the ones she had left behind. From early summer to late fall, the house was never without the strong, sweet aroma of her "white beauties." Papa bought her a stone bench which he placed in the middle of the garden, and she would spend hours sitting, admiring, and talking to her white roses. Sometimes I would joke with Maude that I wondered if they were talking back.

On July 4, 1907, Lizzie's mother, Charlotte Bludworth died and was buried next to her husband, T. W., in Lockhart Cemetery.

This was one of the few times that I saw Lizzie actually grieve. Similar to when her father died, Lizzie mourned alone in her room for several days.

Gussie and Need barely scratched out a living in Lockhart, but poverty didn't stop them from having babies. Three years after they were married, Need Parker "Dick" Jarman, Jr. was born, and a year and a half later, in October 1906, William Harold Jarman was born.

Their marriage was one continuous fight. Neither was happy with how their lives were turning out, and they both blamed the other. In 1909, they separated after seven tumultuous years of marriage and were divorced in 1913.

Several months before the separation, Gussie and her two boys were visiting with us in Meridian when she related that she was worried about her husband. She said that for the past several months he had been acting strangely, and that many nights he would come home stumbling and staggering; he couldn't stand up and would pass out on the sofa. She was worried that something bad was going on with him.

Octavia was in the kitchen but obviously could hear everything that was being said. She cracked the door open and blurted out, "Honey, he ain't sick, he's stone drunk."

Thinking back on that revelation, it seems almost comical, but Gussie had no idea what a drunk was or how one acted. We were taught that alcohol had no place in the life of a good Christian, and never had alcohol been seen in our home. We had never been around anyone who drank, much less someone who drank to excess.

In November 1908, within a month of her visit to Meridian, little William Harold Jarman died of pneumonia at twenty-five months of age. He was buried in the Parker plot with the other Angels of Lockhart Cemetery. When William died, I saw an emotional, grieving side of Gussie that I had never before seen. His death and the realization that she was married to a drunk was more than she could handle. Two months later she left her husband and Mamaw's little cottage in Lockhart and returned to Meridian. She and Dick, now three years old, moved back home to the room she had been so anxious to leave seven years earlier.

Gussie was a changed woman—a twenty-four-year-old mother, beaten down by the stresses of an unhappy marriage. Maturity born of the hardships of life: much more appreciative of the support and love of her father and family.

Gussie would remarry five years later to William Hatton "Billy" Williams, bear him a daughter, Elizabeth, and spend four happy years together before dying in childbirth in 1918, at age thirty-three. She and her stillborn son, William, Jr., would be the last to be buried in the family plot in Lockhart Cemetery, alongside her mother, eight siblings, and a son from her first marriage.

In 1907, my life changed dramatically. I found the love of my life and I left the little city of Meridian and the state of Mississippi behind.

As I mentioned earlier, Lizzie fell in love with the opera and the Grand Opera House, and I have to admit that I thoroughly enjoyed it myself. We spent many a night being entertained by some of the greatest performers in the country. But the opera house was a seasonal occurrence. "The Lady" usually closed for the summer in mid May because it was too hot to sit inside to watch anything, especially with a thousand other people. In fact, the only thing worth doing on most summer evenings was to sit outside on the front porch, with fan in hand, and wish for September to hurry and get here.

The fall concerts were scheduled to start in late September. That year, the first booking for the season was George M. Cohan's Broadway play, *Little Johnny Jones.* It had opened in New York

City in 1904 and featured several songs that are still familiar today: "Give My Regards to Broadway" and "Yankee Doodle Boy." The show had been such a sensational success in New York that a traveling troupe had taken it on tour by train throughout the South and Midwest. We were thrilled that on its way from Chicago to Mobile it was making a stop for a seven-day engagement in Meridian.

For weeks George M. Cohan's show was the talk of the town, and every performance was sold out in advance. Unfortunately, we were only able to get three tickets for the second night's performance. So Papa, who really didn't like all the loud music and the crowds, said that he would stay home with Mamaw and Octavia.

With great anticipation Lizzie, Maude, and I, with Lizzie dressed in her newest and finest, headed out for a wonderful evening of entertainment. The play was great, but the evening was miserable, due to the heat. Usually in late September the evenings are very pleasant, with just a little hint of coolness in the air, but on this evening it was warm and muggy. It must have been eighty-five degrees outside, and inside I couldn't guess. Over a thousand laughing, breathing, sweating bodies were packed into the theatre like sardines, with bright electric lights making it even worse. (The gas lamps had been replaced a few years earlier with light bulbs which seemed to give off more heat than the little gas flames.)

When intermission finally arrived, everyone headed to the exit for some fresh air and a cool glass of water. The man sitting next to me said it was too hot, and he wouldn't be coming back.

As I walked outside, I loosened my collar, looked around, and saw a young boy selling paper fans for a nickel. They were disappearing as fast as he could pull them out of his bag, so I made my way over to him as quickly as I could and handed him a nickel. Without hesitation, he pulled out a fan, handed it to me, and announced that he was all out. Everyone standing around let out a disappointed sigh and walked away.

As I stood there a voice over my shoulder said, "You realize that you cut in front of me. That fan should be mine."

I turned around, and glaring at me was one of the prettiest faces I had ever seen. I was speechless, but finally caught my breath and said, "I'm so sorry. Please, take my fan."

The frown on the face of this young beauty disappeared and a satisfied little smile appeared. "Thanks, and here's your nickel."

"No, no, please keep the money, and again I ask for your forgiveness. It was so thoughtless of me. I usually try to be more of a gentleman, but it's so hot, I wasn't paying attention. I should not have cut in front of you."

She laughed and said, "You're right, it is definitely hot, especially in that room with all those people. You know, it's a shame that we can't just share the fan."

My heart stopped for a moment and I said, "That's a good idea. Please join me. The chair next to me is vacant. The man sitting there said that he would not be back, and I would be honored if you would let me share my fan with you."

"Your fan!" she laughed. "I think you are confused. I believe this is *my* fan."

We both laughed. The rest of that evening was one of the most pleasant, enjoyable times I have ever spent. As for the fan? I didn't need it! In fact, everything that night was wonderful and perfect, even the weather!

This young beauty was Anna Adrienne Therrel. She went by Adrienne. She was from Dallas and had come to the play alone.

After the play was over, I offered to walk her home. To my delight she smiled and said, "That would be very nice. I would enjoy that very much." Her aunt's home was only three blocks from our house.

As we walked, I asked, "If you don't mind me asking, what brings you to Meridian?"

"A few weeks ago," she related, "my family in Dallas received a wire that my Aunt Margaret was very ill. My uncle died several years ago, and they have no children. There's really no family but us, no one else to take care of her. The wire stated that she probably wouldn't last but a few weeks, so I volunteered to come help her in her last days. The next day I caught the train east and have been here caring for her since.

"Before she got sick," Adrienne continued, "Margaret bought a ticket to see *Little Johnny Jones*. She hated to see the ticket go to waste and insisted that I take it and enjoy the evening. Thankfully, one of the neighbors agreed to watch her for a few hours so I could go. And I have to say, this has been an answer to prayer; just to get out of the house for a few hours is a blessing. As she has gotten sicker, caring for her has turned into an around-the-clock task. I know practically no one in Meridian so I came alone. But it has turned into such a wonderful evening."

My heart almost stopped. As we said goodnight, I sheepishly asked, "Would it be okay if I came by tomorrow evening to visit?"

She looked up at me, smiled, and said, "Yes, Oliver, that would be very nice. It gets pretty lonely taking care of my aunt, and a visit would be greatly appreciated."

That night I couldn't sleep. All I could think about was Adrienne. I kept wondering, could she be the one? Early the next morning I got up, ate breakfast, and headed to the depot. I soon found that I couldn't concentrate on anything; the morning and afternoon were just a blur, and I thought the day would never end. I remember several people getting frustrated with me, having to repeat themselves to get my attention. I apologized and said that I wasn't feeling well. On my way home I stopped by to visit Adrienne.

Adrienne met me at the door and introduced me to her aunt, who, even though it was very warm in the house, was sitting in a chair, wrapped in a blanket. She was very sick and coughed constantly. Adrienne said that her aunt was suffering from "consumption"; the way she looked, I wouldn't expect her to last until morning.

Adrienne and I had a very nice visit. She talked about Dallas, the Trinity River, and the vast plains of West Texas. She told me how in the summers the hot winds would blow in from the plains, bringing dust storms that would coat everything with a fine brown powder. And even though the summers were hot, often well over a hundred degrees, it was a dry heat with no humidity, unlike the muggy, stifling summers in Mississippi.

In the middle of our conversation, I heard her say something about being sixteen years old. *Sixteen!* I thought she was kidding. Adrienne couldn't be sixteen years old. She seemed so mature and much older. I would have sworn that she was at least twenty-five years old.

I stopped her in mid conversation, leaned forward, and asked, "How old did you say you were?"

She answered, "Sixteen; but I'll be seventeen in April."

I sat there dumbfounded. Is this proper? Is this wrong? Here I am thirty years old, essentially courting a sixteen year old. I felt guilty. But I thoroughly enjoyed Adrienne's company, and I could sense that she enjoyed mine. I did not want to see our relationship end over such a minor detail as age.

Over the next several weeks, my visits continued and our relationship grew. But her aunt got sicker and sicker. She soon became bed-ridden, unable to get up. Instead of her aunt sitting in the parlor with us, she remained in the bed in the next room. With the modesty of the times, I felt uncomfortable sitting alone with Adrienne. So for decency's sake, I started inviting Maude to accompany me on my visits. I wanted there to be no talk of impropriety, or even a hint of impropriety, when I visited.

Adrienne often joined my family for supper. Toward the end, her aunt ate only soup and broth, and Maude would stay with her aunt so that Adrienne could come over for one of Octavia's delicious home-cooked meals and Mamaw's mouth watering pies.

In early December 1907, Adrienne's aunt finally succumbed to the ravages of consumption, also known as tuberculosis. She was buried in Rose Hill Cemetery on a cold, rainy day, beside her husband of forty years. Attending the burial were Adrienne, Maude, a few neighbors, and myself. Adrienne's aunt had no relatives near, except for Adrienne, and none of the relatives from Texas were able to attend. Even by train, it would have been a couple of days' journey to get here, and the family was not that close anyway.

Two days after the funeral Adrienne announced that it was time for her to go back to Dallas. Her task in Meridian was complete and she needed to get back to her family. Even though I knew that her returning to Dallas was inevitable, it still ripped my heart apart. I couldn't stand the thought of her leaving. I realized that if she left with nothing more than a "good-bye," there was a good chance I would never see her again. It was now or never.

That evening we invited Adrienne over for dinner. Even though she was not leaving for another two days, Octavia prepared a huge farewell feast for our guest. She declared that she was going to do it again tomorrow night. Octavia wanted Adrienne's family to know that she had been treated well in Mississippi. By being "treated well," she meant "fed well." Our guest must go back to Texas a little heavier than when she came. Mamaw made a lemon pie, Adrienne's favorite.

After dinner, we visited for a while in the parlor. I don't remember a thing about that visit; as I look back now, it's just a blur.

My mind was too busy trying to figure out when, where, and how I was going to propose to her. I thought what if she refuses? What if she says she likes me, but more like a brother? She's sixteen years old, I'm thirty; what if she thinks it's funny and starts to laugh? I felt weak and I remember my palms getting all sweaty, even though it was only fifty degrees outside.

My mind was off somewhere when Mamaw said to me, "Aren't you going to walk her home?"

"What?" I asked as I looked around. Everyone was staring at me.

"Adrienne just said that it was time for her to be going home," Mamaw said. "It's gotten dark and a little cool, and I know she doesn't want to walk home by herself."

"Oh, yes, of course," I said, returning to my senses.

Adrienne thanked Octavia and Mamaw for the wonderful meal and thanked us all for being so kind to her over the past few weeks. She said that we had become family to her, she didn't know what she would have done without us, and that she was really going to miss us.

I helped Adrienne with her coat. As we started to walk out, Papa asked, "Ollie, aren't you going to put on your coat? It's rather cold out tonight."

I felt my chest and arms. I had forgotten to put on my coat. Everyone was staring at me. Maude and Mamaw were smiling as if to say, "We know what's on your mind!" I felt my face turn red as I thanked Papa and reached for my coat.

The night was cool and the wind had picked, but it was still comfortable enough for us to take our time. I didn't want to rush her home. She talked about her family and how much she had missed them. It had been almost three months since she had seen them. She couldn't wait to spend Christmas at home with her family in Texas.

I don't think I said a word during the three-block walk to her aunt's home; I was having a hard time just breathing. When we reached her front gate, we paused and I told myself it's time. You've got to do it now!

Adrienne was standing beside me, admiring the Victorian features of her aunt's old home, and commenting on how beautiful it was.

I took a deep breath and turned toward her. I reached for both of her hands and said, "Adrienne, I'm not good at this, I've never done this before." Think, Ollie, think! "But the thought of you going back to Texas is about to break my heart. Ever since we met, I haven't been able to think of anything but you. I've never had feelings like this before, but I know with all my heart that I love you, and I want to spend the rest of my life with you. Will you marry me?"

Adrienne smiled, squeezed my hands, and said, "Oliver, for the past several weeks I have been hoping and praying that you would ask me. I've been sending letters home to my family almost every day, telling them about the wonderful man I met. Yes, Oliver, I would love to marry you." (She always called me Oliver.) "But first, you must come to Dallas and meet my family. You will need to get my father's approval."

That night sleep never came. I was overjoyed, thinking about my future with Adrienne; but I was also very apprehensive. I had never been *anywhere;* I had never even been out of Lauderdale County. The idea of getting on a train and traveling five hundred miles scared me to death. And leaving my family? Why, I had never been away from them for more than a day or two at a time. I guess that I had assumed that she would just marry me on the spot and we would live happily ever after in Meridian, in a little white cottage down the street, and never stray outside the invisible boundary of Lauderdale County. But my love for Adrienne was far greater than my fear of leaving Meridian for a few weeks. Little did I realize that

I would go to Dallas with my bride-to-be, and return to my home in Meridian only to visit.

In mid December 1907, Adrienne and I said good-bye to my family, boarded the train, and began our journey west. On New Year's Day 1908, we were married in the First Methodist Church in Dallas, with family and friends in attendance. Papa and Maude were the only Parker representatives to attend. Lizzie was too busy with holiday activities at the opera house, Gussie was still in Lockhart deep in battle with her rarely sober husband, and Mamaw was getting old and was not well enough to travel. She had developed a cough during Christmas that would not go away, and it was rapidly taking its toll on her. She would have loved to come, but we felt she could not make the two-day train ride and survive.

I fell in love with Dallas. It was similar to Meridian, but much larger. Like Meridian, Dallas was a railroad town. The two main railway systems in the state, the Houston & Central Texas (north and south) and the Texas & Pacific (east and west) intersected here creating an instant boom. It had primarily an agriculture and livestock-based economy (before oil was discovered in the 1930's). I was also surprised to learn that the state of Texas grew more cotton than my home state of Mississippi.

Even though Adrienne was more than willing to return to my home state, Mississippi, to settle, I decided Dallas was to be our home. I had no trouble finding work with the railway system, doing the same thing I was doing in Meridian, telegraphy. I had thought that the change in the level of activity from Lockhart to Meridian was great, but from Meridian to Dallas, it was astounding. The work was monumental and challenging, but I thoroughly enjoyed what I was doing. And I guess having been sheltered in Meridian, I didn't realize how well I had mastered the telegraph and how good I was. Within a few months I was promoted to lead telegrapher.

Adrienne and I settled in to a happy life together in Dallas. But in February 1908, two months after we married, we got a wire from home that made me weak in my knees. "MAMAW SICK, VERY SICK. STOP. DOCTOR SAYS ONLY FEW DAYS. STOP. SHE WANTS YOU TO COME. STOP." That afternoon, Adrienne and I caught the train back to Meridian.

Chapter 31

We arrived in Meridian early Sunday morning, having traveled for thirty-six hours with very little sleep. Papa was waiting at the station with the buggy, and after getting the luggage, we headed home.

"Papa, how is Mamaw doing?" I cautiously asked as we approached the house.

"She's not doing well at all," Papa answered. "Dr. Tatum doesn't expect her to last another twenty-four hours. Ollie, she's been asking for you. She said that she didn't want to die without seeing you."

When we arrived, I went straight to her room. She was lying in bed, with her head and back propped up with pillows. She was coughing and could hardly breathe. She looked so old and pitiful. I wanted to cry, but I knew I couldn't. I didn't want her to see me like that.

"Mamaw, it's Ollie," I said. "I'm home. How are you feeling?"

"Ollie, thank the Lord," she said as she coughed and gasped. "I so wanted to see you. I couldn't die without you being here. Where is your lovely wife?"

"She's here," I said. "She'll be in here in a few minutes. She wanted to freshen up for you."

"I'm sorry I couldn't make the wedding," she continued. "Maude said it was beautiful. You were so handsome and Adrienne such a beauty. Ya'll are going to have a wonderful life together."

Mamaw reached over and took my hand. "Ollie, I'm not doing very well at all. I developed a little cough right after Christmas that I just couldn't get rid of. It's gradually gotten worse, and for the past few days I've been coughing so hard that I can't catch my breath. Dr. Tatum says I've got pneumonia. You know, he is such a fine, caring doctor. He's been coming by twice a day to check on me. I know he's young, but I really like him."

She coughed again and grimaced in pain. "My chest hurts so much when I cough. Dr. Tatum thinks that with all the coughing, I may have cracked some ribs. And I feel so weak and washed out. I don't feel like I have an ounce of energy." She smiled and said, "It's not any fun getting old and sick. But as they say, you either grow old or you die young." She tried to laugh but the laugh turned into a soft cry of pain.

"Mamaw, try to save your energy; you're going to wear yourself out. You don't have to talk. I'll be here."

"No, Ollie, we need to talk. I know I won't be here long. No one will tell me, but I know I can't last. I'm ready to die, but, Ollie, I'm so scared. With all my heart I know that heaven is waiting, that Jesus has saved me and promised me a place at the foot of his throne, but I'm scared. Doubts and fears run through my mind. I have moments where I wonder if there really is a heaven, if there is life beyond this life. And those thoughts scare me to death."

"Mamaw, that's O.K. We all doubt at times, but that's where faith takes over."

"Yes, Ollie," she said as she smiled and rested back on her pillow. "That's what faith is all about. Even though we can't see heaven, can't touch it, we have to believe with all our hearts that it is real, that it is waiting for us. Otherwise life would be so . . . meaningless.

"Ollie," she continued, "this afternoon I was thinking about a song that Fanny Crosby wrote, and I can't remember all the words. But it has brought so much peace to me. '*Safe in the arms of Jesus, safe on His gentle breast.*' And I can't remember the rest of it. Do you remember how it goes? Can you help me with it?"

"Yes, Ma'am," I answered. I began to sing, "*Safe in the arms of Jesus, safe on His gentle breast, There by His love o'ershadowed, sweetly my soul shall rest. Hark! 'Tis the voice of angels, bore in a song to me. Over the field of glory, over the jasper sea.*" My eyes filled with tears as I watched my grandmother smile and say a little prayer.

"Ollie, please make sure they sing that song for me."

"Yes, Ma'am, I will."

Mamaw paused for a moment to catch her breath. "Ollie," she said, "as I've lain here over the past few days, I've thought so much about the past twenty-two years. The years have flashed by so fast. It seems like only yesterday when your Mama died, and when your Papa came to Meridian, wanting me to move to Lockhart to help raise you and your sisters. You and Maude have done so well; you with your dots and dashes and Maude with her music. I'm so proud of the two of you. And I'm not going to give up on Gussie. I keep praying that her life will straighten out. Ollie, I often wonder if her twin sister, Cornelia, had lived, would Gussie have been different. If having to learn to share, to give and take with another . . . But we will never know."

She coughed again and struggled for breath. Tears welled up in her eyes, and she began to cry softly. "I think about those little Angels in Lockhart Cemetery: Stephen, Timothy, Hugh Lee, Roger, and those two precious little girls, Gena and Elizabeth. My heart aches so much. Six precious little babies. Oh, how I wish that things had been different. Stephen would be almost seventeen years old now. I know he would have been such a handsome young man. It hurts to think about it."

I couldn't say anything. I knew I would have broken down and cried like a baby. Tears filled my eyes. I couldn't let myself think about those babies.

"And, Ollie, you and I have been so close. Through the years, we've shared our innermost thoughts with each other, bared our very hearts and souls. We've had a bond that very few people ever experience and have shared thoughts that we could not share with anyone else." She shifted in bed again, unsuccessfully trying to find a comfortable position. Her voice softened, "There is something we have to talk about. Ollie," she whispered, "Lizzie is pregnant; she's going to have another baby."

Suddenly, in an instant, the sadness and sorrow that I was experiencing changed to utter shock. Lizzie pregnant? That can't be! Mamaw has to be wrong!

"She's about three or four months along; she thinks she's due in July. She and your Papa have known for a month or two, but didn't tell anyone until about a week ago. Papa said that he was going to send you a wire about it, but with my getting so sick, he never got around to it."

"Mamaw, I don't know what to say or think. I just can't believe it! Lizzie will be forty years old next month, and Papa is fifty-six. I thought that little Elizabeth was their last."

"That's what we all thought," Mamaw replied. "Maude and Octavia were just as shocked as you are. They are so upset. When Papa told Octavia, she nodded politely, but then went up to her room, shut the door, and cried for an hour."

"What was Papa's reaction?" I asked, still numb from the news.

"He hasn't really said anything else about it," Mamaw answered. "He just told us the news, kind of matter of fact, without any emotion at all. I can usually read my son's face, but this time, I couldn't. He didn't seem overjoyed, but he didn't seem distraught either. I couldn't tell what he was thinking. And Lizzie. She hasn't said a single word about it, not even a hint. She has gone on with all her activities as if nothing at all was different. I just don't know what to think."

Mamaw coughed repeatedly, gasped for breath, and grimaced in pain. She then wretched, almost choking, and coughed again, but this time she coughed up some blood. She settled back on her pillows trying to catch her breath. I reached for a towel, moistened it in a basin of water next to the bed, and gently wiped her face. She reached over, patted me on the knee, and smiled.

"Mamaw, don't try to talk anymore. You need to rest. We can talk a little later when you're feeling better."

She rose up slowly on her elbows, caught her breath, and said, "No, Ollie, we need to talk now. I'm not going to get better. I'm going to die, and we have got to talk about Lizzie and this baby."

The reality of her sickness, and the fact that she was not going to get well, rushed back into my mind, but it did not overshadow the thoughts of Lizzie and a baby. I knew Mamaw was right. We had to talk. Time was too short and I needed her guidance.

"Ollie, I'm so worried about this baby," Mamaw continued, struggling for breath. "When Elizabeth died five years ago, I thought that she was the last, and I didn't think there was any use in doing anything. I asked you then, what could we do? The child was dead, and nothing would bring her back. To start making accusations would have done nothing but bring heartache and embarrassment to the family. Putting Lizzie in jail or the lunatic asylum would have accomplished nothing."

"Mamaw, what can I do?" I asked.

"I don't know, Ollie. You know as well as I do that there is no way to prove that she was the cause of a single death. Why, we don't even have evidence that she harmed any of them. But if this baby suffers the same fate as its six little brothers and sisters, I don't think I will ever be able to rest peacefully in my grave. As I lie here dying, I can't think of anything else. I've thought about it day and night. It has consumed me more that the thought of actually dying. We have to do something."

"Mamaw, I'll speak to Papa. I think that's the best thing to do. He is not blind to what has happened. He'll have to address our concerns somehow. I would bet that he's concerned right now and is considering how to handle it."

"I'm not sure what he thinks, or even if he'll *let* himself think about it," Mamaw replied, her voice weak and her breathing shallow. "You spoke to him when you were concerned about little Elizabeth, and he did nothing."

"Yes, but things are different now. Another baby died, and he has to be concerned, and he has to know he must do something. He can't ignore the past now. He can't just stand by and let another baby die!"

Mamaw eased back down on her pillows, holding her chest as she coughed. "It hurts so much when I cough; I feel like my ribs are breaking." She then took a shallow breath and relaxed as best she could. "Ollie, I do hope that your father will listen and be as concerned as we are. The thought of another baby dying . . . I can't bear it. Thank you for talking with him.

"And thank you and Adrienne for coming," she continued. "I will rest easier knowing that you are here. You know, I've missed having you around. Just the other day I was thinking that for the past twenty-two years, until two months ago, we have visited together almost every single day." She smiled weakly. "I used to love when you would come by after school for a slice of apple pie or peach cobbler. My, you had an appetite! Watching you grow from a scrawny eight-year-old to a fine young man . . . it has been such a joy. And now, a fine husband! I'm so proud of you. And such a wonderful, beautiful wife!"

Mamaw coughed repeatedly, then caught her breath, and continued, "For the first month you were gone, I wished that you and Adrienne would move back home, back to Meridian, so we would be close. But I now see that's not to be, not what God has in His plans for you, or for me. I know that He has greater plans for you than I could have ever have imagined or hoped for."

She paused again, gasped for breath, and whispered, "Promise me again that you will talk to your Papa. Tell him how concerned we are about Lizzie and this baby. Tell him that he has to do something."

There was a knock on the door behind me, and Adrienne and Maude quietly walked in. Maude's eyes were red and swollen; she was having little success in trying not to cry. Adrienne sat down on the side of the bed, picked up Mamaw's hand and kissed it gently. We sat silently as Mamaw drifted off to sleep.

"Yes, Mamaw, I promise," I whispered.

At ten o'clock that night, Mamaw died in her sleep. Two days later she was buried in Lockhart Cemetery next to her husband, who had been waiting patiently for her for twenty-five years.

Chapter 32

Adrienne and I decided to stay for a few days visit. I needed time to think, and I needed to talk to Papa.

The day after the funeral, Adrienne and I took the buggy and rode back to Lockhart. The only time that Adrienne had been to Lockhart was the day of Mamaw's funeral, and we had not had time to visit. I wanted her to see where I had spent most of my life.

I showed her the house where I grew up; it was hard to believe that I had been gone from that old place for six years. I hardly recognized Mamaw's little cottage down the road. Gussie and the boys weren't there; she was still in Meridian after the funeral, not ready to come back to face her problems. The cottage was a mess, run down; the floor on the front porch, almost rotted away. The place looked worse than it did before we rescued it twenty-two years ago for Mamaw.

We stopped by the depot and I introduced Adrienne to my old crew. Everyone looked the same, except for a little grey hair on some and a little less on others. We stopped by and visited with Junius. He was doing well with the farm, living alone since his mother had died last year. Junius hadn't married and wasn't looking. He said that his brother James was doing well in Jackson, but that he hadn't seen him since their mother's funeral. He smiled as he said that James had married two years ago and had a little girl named Charlotte.

The last place we stopped was Lockhart Methodist Church and the cemetery. I showed Adrienne where Mama was buried. I told her about how wonderful and beautiful Mama was, how close we were, and how I still missed my Mama. I told her about little Cornelia, Gussie's twin sister who is buried to the left of Mama, and how I barely remembered her.

Then we looked to the right of Mama and I introduced her to each of the little angels: Stephen, Timothy, Hugh Lee, Roger, Gena, and Elizabeth. I tried to tell her everything that I could remember about their short-lived lives. I wanted her to know them. Lastly I told her about their deaths, about my concerns for Lizzie's unborn child, and about my conversation with Mamaw before she died.

Tears filled my eyes, and I began to choke up. Adrienne quietly moved over to me, embraced me gently, and kissed me on the cheek. "Ollie, I love you so much," she said, "and I will be praying for you, praying that you will know just what to say to your Papa."

We got back in the buggy and began the two and a half hour journey back to Meridian. It was almost three-thirty on this February day, and it would be dark when we got home.

The next morning I woke up early. I didn't sleep much that night, thinking about what I was going to say to Papa. I dressed quickly and went downstairs; I hoped to talk with him before he left for work.

When I got downstairs, Octavia was in the kitchen, cooking breakfast. "Octavia, where's Papa?" I asked.

"He's gone, Mr. Ollie," Octavia answered. "He left without a bite, only grabbed a cup of coffee. He said that since you and Miss Adrienne are leaving tomorrow, he wanted to get to the office early and get finished by lunch time. He plans to take the afternoon off and visit with ya'll this afternoon. Have a seat," she said as she reached for the coffee pot. "The coffee is hot and breakfast will be ready in just a few minutes."

"I'm not hungry," I said as I sat down, "but I will take some coffee."

"Mr. Ollie, you are at least going to have some biscuits," Octavia insisted. "They'll be out of the oven in just a few minutes, and I'm not going to let you go hungry this morning."

I took a sip of coffee, looked up at Octavia, and asked, "How have you been doing over the past few days? Are you making it all right?"

Octavia began to cry. "Mr. Ollie, I don't know how I'm going to get along without Miz Parker. She and I had become so close. Why, she was like a sister to me, treated me like part of the family instead of like hired help. I'm really going to miss her and," she smiled, "and her wonderful pies."

I took another sip of coffee. "I hear Lizzie is going to have another baby. Mamaw told me the other night before she died." I paused for a moment, and then asked, "Tell me what you think about the news."

She shook her head and said, "I have never been so upset in all my life than when I found out that Miz Lizzie was pregnant again. How in the world could they have let that happen? Doesn't your Papa have any sense at all? Why, the last thing in this world they need is a baby. I've been so upset about it that I can't see straight."

As she spoke, her voice got louder and louder. She paused, suddenly embarrassed at what she had just said. She lowered her head, turned to the sink, and quietly said, "But then, I'm only the hired help. I need to remember my place and I shouldn't be giving my opinion on what your Papa and Miz Lizzie are doing."

As I was finishing my coffee and a biscuit, Lizzie walked in, poured herself a cup of coffee, and headed for the door. "I'll be home around two o'clock," she said, halfway out the door. "The Opera House Auxiliary is having a planning meeting this morning for our spring social, and then a luncheon, and I just cannot miss it. Ollie, before you and Adrienne leave, I want to give you some cuttings from my rose bushes. With those hot summers in Dallas, you should have beautiful roses in no time, as long as you keep them well watered. See ya'll later."

As she left, Octavia frowned, shook her head, and said, "I'm not going to say a thing . . . I'm not going to say a thing."

Papa came home at twelve-thirty, happy to have the rest of the day off. Octavia had prepared a wonderful lunch for us. As we sat at the table, I was too anxious to eat, worried about finding a good opportunity to talk to Papa. Octavia fussed at me for just pushing my food around on the plate, and said she didn't want me to head off to Texas hungry, and I couldn't leave without at least a few extra pounds around my waist.

After lunch, Papa and I excused ourselves to the porch while Octavia, Maude, and Adrienne cleared off the table and took care of the dishes. Although it was mid-February, the weather was mild, the temperature in the low sixties, without a hint of a breeze. It was perfect for sitting and visiting.

Papa was sitting in Mamaw's old rocker and slowly began to rock. "The weather's been unusually mild this winter," he said, "one of the mildest we've had in years. I've always felt that we need at least one good freeze, if for no other reason, to kill the bugs."

"Yes, sir," I said, "I bet the bugs and mosquitoes will be a big problem this summer."

We continued to talk about the weather for a while, and then we talked about Dallas. I told him about my work and how well things were going for Adrienne and me. Papa said that when he and Maude came for the wedding, he was really impressed with

Dallas. It seemed to be a great place to live and raise a family. He was glad that things were falling into place for me.

He continued to rock in Mamaw's old rocker. The familiar creak reminded me of how much I would miss my grandmother.

After a few minutes I said, "Papa, it just doesn't seem right without Mamaw here. We are really going to miss her."

Papa nodded his head in agreement and replied, "Yes, we will. She has been such an important part of our family for the past twenty years, and it's really going to take some adjusting to fill the void she has left. We are all going to miss her, but I know that you will probably miss her most. The two of you had developed such a close bond. After your mother died, she stepped right in and became the mother that you needed. I know that Lizzie never really filled that role for you like she did for the girls. It was good that Mamaw was there for you."

After a short pause, I said, "Mamaw told me about Lizzie being pregnant. How is she feeling?"

"She's doing well," he answered. "For a while there she was fairly puny with the morning sickness, but now at about four months, she is feeling great and back to all her usual activities."

"Papa, what do you think about the pregnancy?" I cautiously asked.

He was silent for a few seconds and then said, "Initially, I was a bit surprised and shocked."

Come on Papa, I thought, you know how it works! What were you thinking?

"But now I'm pretty excited about it and looking forward to July. I sure hope I can keep up with this new arrival. You know, I'm almost fifty-six!"

There was a short pause in the conversation, and I knew it was now or never. This might be the only opportunity I would have to get it out in the open.

"Papa, yesterday Adrienne and I took the buggy and rode up to Lockhart. She had never really seen our little community except for the day of Mamaw's funeral, and I wanted her to get to know the town I grew up in. While we were there, we went to the cemetery and I showed her where Mama is buried and told her how wonderful she was and how much I miss her. I then showed her where all the babies are buried. I told her everything I could remember about each one of them: I want her to know them and love them the way we did. Those babies were so sweet and beautiful. It breaks my heart to think about them. And with Mamaw's death, I have been thinking about them a lot.

"You know, if Stephen were alive, he would be seventeen years old, almost grown. I think of how different things might have been. And I've been thinking back on each of their lives and their deaths and how traumatic those times were for our family. Stephen and that horrible cough, Timothy and the typhoid fever; it was so hard to stand by and watch those two babies just waste away. And Roger's accident, the scalding; such a horrible death. And then I look at Hugh Lee, Gena, and Elizabeth; no explanation, absolutely none. With each of their deaths, I became more and more uncomfortable with the explanation that it 'just happened.'"

I paused for a moment. Papa had been silent and remained so.

I took a deep breath and continued. "Papa, I'm sorry, but I just cannot stand by and say nothing. When I heard that Lizzie was pregnant again, I couldn't believe it. I don't think I have ever been so shocked in all my life. And Papa, I'm worried about this new baby. I worry that it will suffer the same fate as the other six, and we just cannot allow that to happen. Something has to be done to insure that this baby does not end up in Lockhart Cemetery with its brothers and sisters." My voice was quivering. "Our family cannot let another baby die. It would be unforgivable."

As I finished, my voice was quivering. My hands were trembling and sweaty and I was out of breath. I stood there, shaking, quietly waiting for a response.

Papa sat still for a few moments, then rose slowly. He walked to the front of the porch and placed his hands on the railing, standing there as I had seen him stand a hundred times before when he was deep in thought. He looked out into the yard, and after what seemed an hour, he turned and looked at me. His eyes were moist. He had a look on his face that silently pleaded, begged for help.

He then said, "Ollie, what would you propose that I do?" He reached into his pocket, pulled out a handkerchief, and wiped away the tears. He slowly turned around, placed his hands back on the rail again, and stared out into the yard.

His response caught me off guard. There was no denial from him that there was a problem; no trying to explain away the deaths; only an obvious admission that he was as concerned and as worried as I was.

And then I thought, what would I propose that Papa do? What would *I* do? What were the options? As I sat there, it suddenly hit me that the answer to that question was horribly more difficult than I had ever imagined. What would I do? Would I take this newborn from Lizzie? Would I have him reared by someone else, far away from his mother? Give the baby to Adrienne and me to raise? To Gussie and Need? Would I try to have her committed to a lunatic asylum, put away so that she would never be near the baby again? Why, she is just as sane as I am! Would I leave the baby with her, allow her to raise this baby, be his mother, but never leave him alone with her? An impossible task. Would I talk to the sheriff and put the decision in the hands of the court? But it's been almost five years since Elizabeth died. Why didn't we go to the authorities then? And remember, there was absolutely no evidence at all that these deaths were anything but innocent. Would I talk to the minister and seek guidance from him? What advice could he possibly give that I had not already thought of?

Then I thought, would I approach Lizzie and accuse her? But what good would that do? If she denies it, what would I do? Ignore her denial and take the baby away? If she admits it and fervently says that it will never happen again, do I believe her? I sat there, totally dumbfounded. I did not have an answer. I did not know what to do.

I stood up, walked over to Papa, put my hand on his shoulder, and said, "Papa, I don't know. I don't know what to do."

Papa turned around and said, "Neither do I."

That night I did not sleep at all. I kept thinking and worrying, realizing how much my father was suffering and how much he had endured, and I had nothing to offer; no advice for him that would make things right. My heart ached as I realized that tomorrow Adrienne and I would leave Meridian behind, leaving my father with no plan for handling this potentially horrible situation. I thought about Mamaw, how much I needed her words of wisdom. I prayed fervently through the night that God Almighty would give Papa the wisdom and the strength to know the right thing to do.

The weather changed abruptly during the night. A cold front came raging through, pushing out the mild temperatures and bringing in icy rain and bitter wind. We were quickly reminded that it was the middle of February and still winter. The next morning the wind continued to howl as we loaded up the buggy. After tearful goodbyes and hugs, Adrienne, Papa, and I bundled up as well as we could against the cold, driving rain and headed to the depot. Papa and I unloaded the luggage.

For several minutes, Adrienne and I stood on the loading ramp, waiting until the last minute to board the train. I looked at Papa. He was shivering in the cold: stooped over, bracing himself against the wind. He looked so old. I prayed: Dear God, how will he get through the next few months? How will he handle this new baby? And more terrifying, how will he handle the fear that this baby may die?

The freezing rain suddenly changed to sleet. "Papa, it looks like you may get that freeze after all."

"Yes, son, I think we will."

The conductor came by and said it was time to board. We embraced and said good-bye.

"Papa, I'll miss you," I said.

"And I'll miss you, too, son."

As I started to walk away, I paused and turned back. "Papa, I love you more than you will ever know, and I'll be praying for you with all my heart and soul."

With tears in his eyes, he thanked me, climbed back in the buggy, and headed home, to his wife.

ALTON BYRON
PARKER
Son of
Mr. & Mrs.
S.D. Parker

Born
July 24, 1908
Died
May 22, 1910
Age 22 Mo., 1 Day

Another little angel
Before the heavenly throne

The End

Epilogue

In 1951, an odd illness, *Munchausen's Syndrome,* was described in which a patient would cause himself to be ill or would fake an illness for the purpose of gaining attention. In extreme cases people have been known to ingest poisons and seriously injure themselves in order to get attention. Munchausen's syndrome is different from hypochondria, a condition in which the patient seeks medical care because he "thinks" he is ill. In Munchausen's Syndrome the sole reason for the malingering is to gain attention. (The term Munchausen was derived from Karl Friedrich Hieronymus, Freiherr von Munchausen, a German Baron, a dignitary of the eighteenth century, known for exaggerating stories and tales about his life. His tall tales included riding cannon balls during battle, going to the moon, and pulling himself out of quicksand by grabbing his own hair. His stories are still very popular among children in the Russian states.)

Munchausen's by Proxy is similar to Munchausen's, but in this case the person gains attention by inducing, or faking, illness in *someone else.* The classic case is a mother who fabricates or induces illness in a young child, takes the child from doctor to doctor, appearing to be extremely concerned for their "sick" child. These children are often subjected to multiple tests and procedures, and sometimes even surgery to try to find the "cause" of their illness. Quite often, the mother is in the medical field, knowledgeable enough about medical conditions and their symptoms to keep doctors totally in the dark. Victims have been known to be poisoned, have bones broken, and even be murdered to satisfy the need for attention by the caregiver. (In the movie *The Sixth Sense,* one of the dead children was ultimately found to be the victim of poisoning by a parent, with the parent reaping sympathy and attention from the child's "sickness" and ultimate death.)

(Sources: E-Medicine—Munchausen Syndrome, by William Ernoehazy; SIDS-Network.org)

That being said, I want to make it perfectly clear that I have no evidence that any of the Parker babies in Lockhart Cemetery were victims of Munchausen's by Proxy. In fact I have no knowledge of how any of the babies died. As far as we know, every death was well-explained, due to the ravages of disease in a time when medicine usually did more harm than good. But I can't help wondering and imagining. My wife says that when I get to heaven, Lizzie, with all her babies in tow, is going to meet me at the Pearly Gates, shake her finger at me, and say "Shame on you, Thomas Wiley!"

But suppose this story has some truth to it; suppose a question had been raised that these deaths were not "natural," but were murder, committed to gain attention and sympathy. Then why was nothing done? How could the family and the community stand by and not do something? Where were the authorities?

Realize that in that time there was *no* child advocacy, no child social workers, and no place to report the abuse of children. In fact, the Fair Labor Standard Acts which limited child labor was not passed until 1938. Child abuse in its many forms was very rarely dealt with, and then usually just within the family. The thought of a non-family member, authority or not, interfering with how a parent treated or dealt with a child was often grounds for pulling out the shotgun.

Child advocacy is a very new phenomenon, and child abuse is still very difficult to report, investigate, and correct. I would suppose that if any of the Parker family or friends had suspected that the deaths of these little ones were unnatural, it would have been handled very quietly and probably just swept under the rug. Then, as now, families will go to great lengths, even turning their backs on the deaths of children, to prevent a scandal in the family from becoming public. But again, I have no information that would suggest that these little ones died of anything but the evil diseases of childhood.

Although the day-to-day activities and thoughts of the characters in this story are fabricated, the actual people and places are not. The main characters all really existed. Their birthdates, ages, dates of marriages and deaths are accurate. Names of the minor characters were family names or were names "lifted" off gravestones in Lockhart Cemetery.

I tried to portray the personalities of the characters as true to how they really were as I could. You may wonder how that was possible since they had been dead for over fifty years. One source was my father-in-law, Arthur Simpson Coburn, Jr. (son of Maude Parker Coburn). He was a great storyteller, and for years had told Merrie about family members, their lives, their idiosyncrasies, and their peculiarities. Another wonderful source was Merrie's eighty-seven-year-old aunt, Hazel Augusta "Gussie" Coburn Riggan, and her husband, Hodges Riggan, who had a wealth of information about Lizzie, Stephen, Ollie, and all the other family members—information that I was able to use to formulate their characters. One of Uncle Hodges' comments was that the Parker family was "very strange." Sadly, Aunt Gussie died in September 2006, while I was writing this book.

The narrator of the story, Oliver "Ollie" Eras Parker, was a telegrapher and lived his adult life in the Dallas area. When and where he and his wife, Adrienne met and married, no one knows. They had three children and then divorced. Ollie died in 1944 and, interestingly, is buried in Magnolia Cemetery in Meridian next to Lizzie and Stephen. His wife, Adrienne, I assume, is buried in Texas. Also, contrary to the story, Ollie must have had a very good and loving relationship with Lizzie because he named one of his daughters Elizabeth and his son Stephen Decatur II. Ollie lost an arm at some point in time, but no one recalls the circumstances. In the family picture, notice that his left shoulder appears much smaller than the right.

You may realize that Ollie could not really have been the narrator, because the narration is set in 1952, and he had died eight years earlier. But I felt that he was the best character to tell the story.

I know very little about Mamaw, Augusta Byron Parker, except that she died in 1904 at age seventy-five. She and her husband John Woods Parker, Sr., who was twenty-two years older than his wife, had three children. She and her husband were lifelong residents of Lockhart and, as far as I know, never lived in Meridian. Before the Civil War, the Parker family had a plantation in the Lockhart area, but no one knows any of the details. They are buried in Lockhart Cemetery only a few feet from their grandbabies.

Lizzie's character is very true to how she really was. According to Merrie's aunt and uncle, Lizzie was very social conscious and involved in the social scene of Meridian. She liked to entertain and to be entertained. "Uppity" was the word that was used to describe her. However, according to Merrie's older cousins who remember her in her old age, she was a very kind "doting" great-grandmother, a lot like Mamaw in my story. And contrary to the story, she never seemed to be "crazy," irrational, or out of touch with reality. I don't have any glimpse of how she handled the deaths of her children because they all died before Arthur and Gussie (Merrie's father and aunt) were born. (Notice that in the family picture, Lizzie is holding a white rose.)

Papa was also true to his character, but was called "Big Daddy" rather than Papa. I didn't call him "Big Daddy" because to me it gives the feel of a controlling, in charge, head of the household, like Big Daddy in Tennessee Williams' *Cat on a Hot Tin Roof.* I didn't see him as having that kind of personality. But he was a very successful businessman and very much part of the "movers and shakers" of Meridian at that time. His brother, John, Jr., was mayor of Meridian in the early part of the twentieth century, during the "heyday" of the city's existence. (The present City Hall, built in 1914, and currently undergoing a two-and-a-half-year multimillion-dollar renovation, was built under John's watch. His picture hangs just inside the entrance. According to Ken Storms, Chief Administrative Officer for the city, John's ghost is known to wander the upper floors of the City Hall.)

According to the family, Gussie was spoiled, and it appeared to be Big Daddy's fault. He gave her whatever she wanted and allowed her to pretty much do as she pleased. She and Need Jarman actually did elope and had two sons. He was a heavy drinker and she did divorce him. She returned home and lived with her parents for several years before marrying William Hatton "Billy" Williams. They had one daughter, Elizabeth, named after Lizzie. As with Ollie, she must have had a very good relationship with Lizzie to name a child after her. Gussie died in 1918, at age thirty-three, of childbirth complications. She and her stillborn son were the last to be buried in the Parker plot in Lockhart Cemetery. (We were able to locate the divorce proceeding between Gussie and Need at the Lauderdale County Courthouse, which gave a very detailed account of their tumultuous marriage and life together.)

There were three characters that my wife actually knew: Maude (her grandmother, Clelia Maude Parker Coburn), Octavia, and "Uncle Junius" Bludworth. What she remembers about Uncle Junius is that he fought in World War I, walked with a limp, and had a glass eye. He never married and lived for several years in Meridian with his sister, Lizzie, before she died in 1952. Junius died in 1965 and is buried in Lockhart Cemetery in the Bludworth plot, beside his parents, T. W. and Charlotte, and three brothers, James, John, and Thomas, and sister, Lottie. (It is assumed that these children never married, since they were all buried without spouses in the family plot.)

The other brother, Timothy, is buried next to his wife in Magnolia Cemetery in Meridian near where Stephen, Lizzie, and Ollie are buried.

Maude died in 1957 when Merrie was six years old. She was true to her character—a loving wife, mother, and grandmother. She was an accomplished pianist and began playing in church at age thirteen. She actually did attend Meridian Female College, which no longer exists. As far as we know, she was the first of the Parker family to ever attend college. She and Merrie's grandfather, Arthur Simpson Coburn, Sr., were married for forty-six years.

Octavia was a "member of the family" forty years later than in the book. She was the housekeeper for Merrie's grandparents in the 1940's and 1950's. The book is true to her real character and history; too interesting a person not to include.

Dr. H. F. Tatum was a physician in Meridian at the turn of the century and was the family's physician for years. Dr. Tatum's signature is on Gussie's death certificate of 1918. My father-in-law,

Arthur Coburn, Jr., who was born in 1911, remembered Dr. Tatum standing at the end of his bed when he had whooping cough at age four and telling his parents that he doubted he would live until morning. Thankfully, he did.

If I have offended anyone, family or not, by dragging the late Lizzie Bludworth Parker through the "literary" dirt, I wish to formally apologize; and once again, I emphasize that this story is fabricated . . . but I wonder!

Acknowledgments

On September 15, 2001, four days after our nation's worst disaster, my own personal 9-11 occurred when my oldest son died unexpectedly. In an instant, the sorrow that I was experiencing for my nation disappeared and was replaced by my own personal grief.

For several months after his death, I read numerous books on death and grief; stories of how to continue life in the face of tragedy and loss. Most were written by people who wished to share their own experience of sorrow. Many of the stories were tributes to loved ones. Some were bitter tales of loss and guilt, tragic stories of how the writer wished he could go back and mend a broken relationship, but now it was too late. Most tried to give their formula for dealing with grief.

All of the stories seemed to have one common theme: the writings were cathartic. In the final pages of each book, one could sense a cleansing, a feeling that in writing about his loss, the author felt better. The tragedy had changed him and had affected him deeply—the way he thought, the way he prayed, the way he viewed life. The change was forever; but as he finished his story, he could now go on with his life.

For almost five years, I toyed with writing down my thoughts of death and grief. But the more I read other people's stories, the more I realized that there was nothing of substance that I could add to what had already been written. But I still felt a need to write, a need for my own catharsis.

My visit to the cemetery in Lockhart in January 2006, gave me what I needed: my opportunity to write. This book is my catharsis, my cleansing, as I tell the world of my experience. However, it's written differently than most stories of personal sorrow; it is not *my* story; it's Ollie's story. Through his character I have been able to vicariously express my feelings, the hurts, the doubts, the fears, the anger, and the faith; and at the same time write a story of fiction, based on fact, that has not only been therapeutic for me, but I hope entertaining, suspenseful, and maybe even helpful to you.

This book would not have been written without the support and encouragement of many friends and family members. Once the first draft was completed, the recommendations on how to make it better were invaluable. Thanks to all of you for your contributions.

To my son, David and my daughter-in-law, Elaine, who in the early stages of the book said, "There's a good story in there trying to come out," and "Commas, don't be afraid of commas." To my daughters, Julie Wiley and Betsy Reese, and to my son-in-law, Brent, with pencil in hand, who were my very early critics.

To Larry Goldstein, who read the first chapter and was honest enough to tell me it needed some work. To Dick Brown, Merrie's cousin, who provided several of the family pictures and who was the first "editor." His encouragement kept me going in the early stages of the work. (His grandmother was Gussie.)

To Bob Pittman, for his words of encouragement and his suggestion to build the story into a true mystery. To Teri Blackstock, for her advice to "show the story rather than tell it." What a tremendous difference that made! To Melanie Coburn Daily, Steve Parker Coburn, and Keith Coburn, Merrie's cousins, for their insight, encouragement, and helpful recommendations in making the story better. (Maude was their grandmother.)

To my mother, Pearl Wiley, for her encouragement. To my sisters, Linda Bowlin, Lera Triplett, and Ellen White, and my sister-in-law, Debbie Wiley, for their input and recommending that I change the title to *The Angels of Lockhart* and leave off the word, *Cemetery*. To Jean Butler, Jane Taylor, and Gladys Bowlin, my school teacher aunts, for helping me realize that my writing wasn't bad, after all. To Uncle Hodges Riggan and the late Hazel Augusta "Gussie" Riggan, thank you for the stories and insight into your family's past.

To Nan Sugg, Darden North, and Debbie Dabbs for their advice on publishing. To Rexine Henry, the first "non-family member" to read the manuscript; you were my first "test." Thank you so much for your encouraging comments. To Merrie's luncheon club, *Les Amies,* who were the first to hear a public reading of the book. Their positive response was so welcomed. To Vickie Moss, for helping me see deeper into the characters and for showing me the rose that Lizzie was holding in the family picture.

To Merrie's cousin, Ann Wilson Hayes, Chancery Clerk of Lauderdale County, for the fascinating old family documents that she uncovered on the dusty shelves of the court house. To Dalma Grissom, who provided the history of Hawkins Memorial Methodist Church. Thanks for the tour. To Jack Shank and his book *Meridian, the Queen with a Past*. What a wonderful source of information about your home town.

To Dennis Mitchell, professor at Mississippi State University, Meridian Campus, for the information on the Opera House. To Gayla Bridges, for her help with grammar and punctuation. To Jennifer Welsch, Sue Bray, and the crew at BookMasters, for guiding this first-time author through the steps of publishing, a process that can be quite intimidating.

During the refinement, there were several others who were kind to read the manuscript: Meredith Travelstead, Brenda Scott, Ann Giompoletti, Kathy Robbins, Elisha Matvey, Katherine Wiley, Ricky Robinson, Gina Scott, Trish Ratcliff, Toni Bryant, Terrie Whatley, Donna Burrough, and Judy Tharpe. Your input and encouragement was invaluable.

And last, but definitely not least, to Merrie, my bride of thirty-four years. You were my sounding board, my number one critic and encourager. Thanks for the hours of reading and rereading and your insistence for accuracy, making sure that all the facts were right. Thank you for listening when I know you were tired of me talking about "the book." "The book" is as much yours as it is mine. And thanks for letting me suggest that there are evil skeletons in your family's closet.

Scripture quotations are from the King James Version of the *Holy Bible*. Other quotations are from the *Book of Common Prayer,* 1929 Edition.

Appendix A

The following are the exact inscriptions on each grave marker in the Parker plot in Lockhart Cemetery and are listed in order of burial

1. CORNELIA JEWEL
   DAUGHTER OF
   S. D. & G. S. PARKER
   DIED
   OCT. 29, 1885
   AGED
   10 MOS., 28 DAYS
   GONE SO SOON
2. GEORGIA S. PARKER
   WIFE OF
   S. D. PARKER
   BORN
   FEB. 23, 1860
   DIED
   JULY???1886 (day unreadable)
   AS A WIFE DEVOTED
   AS A MOTHER AFFECTIONATE
   AS A FRIEND EVER KIND AND TRUE

3. STEPHEN DECATUR
   SON OF
   S.D. & LIZZIE J. PARKER
   DIED
   MAY 8, 1890
   AGED
   1 YR., 3 M., 29 DS
   OUR LOVED ONE

4. TIMOTHY WOODS
   SON OF S. D. & L. J. PARKER
   DIED
   SEPT. 15, 1891
   AGED
   1 YR. 15 DYS.
   GONE TO A BETTER LAND

5. HUGH LEE
   SON OF
   S. D. & LIZZIE J. PARKER
   DIED
   MAY 27, 1897
   AGED
   1 YR., 4 M., 6 DS.
   ONLY SLEEPING

6. ROGER LLOYD
   SON OF
   S. D. & L. J. PARKER
   DIED
   SEPT. 6, 1899
   AGED
   1 YR., 7 MOS., 5 DAYS
   GONE TO BE AN ANGEL

7. EUGENIA
   DAUGHTER OF
   S.D. & LIZZIE
   PARKER
   BORN
   FEB. 4, 1890
   DIED
   OCT. 31, 1901
   SWEET BABE THY SPIRIT
   (See footnote 4)

8. ELIZABETH
   DAUGHTER OF
   S. D. & ELIZABETH
   PARKER
   BORN MAY 18, 1902
   DIED APRIL 1, 1903
   WE WILL MISS YOU

9. Wm HAROLD
   JARMAN
   BORN OCT. 5, 1906
   DIED NOV. 19, 1908

10. ALTON BYRON
    PARKER
    SON OF
    MR. & MRS.
    S. D. PARKER
    BORN
    JULY 24, 1908
    DIED
    MAY 22, 1910
    AGE 22 MO., 1 DAY
    ANOTHER LITTLE ANGEL
    BEFORE THE HEAVENLY THRONE

11. MOTHER
    MARY AUGUSTA
    WIFE OF
    W. H. WILLIAMS
    DEC. 6, 1884
    FEB. 12, 1918
    SHE WAS A KIND AND AFFECTIONATE WIFE
    A FOND MOTHER AND A FRIEND TO ALL

12. WHWJr[5]

Notes

1. The home on 25th Avenue in Meridian is now gone, but the old brick general store still stands, empty and silent.

2. According to the current Mayor of Union, Max Sessums, great nephew of Ma Sessums, the old Sessums/Parker Hotel burned to the ground in the early 1990's.

3. The doors of the Grand Opera House remained shut, untouched and undisturbed, until the beginning of the twenty-first century, when a multimillion dollar renovation was undertaken to revive the original beauty of "The Lady." In the fall of 2006, it was reopened, almost eighty years after her closure.

4. If you are a "detail" reader, you may have noticed in Appendix A that the grave marker for Eugenia (#7) states that she was born February 4, 1890, making her 11 years old when she died, not 20 months. However, this date doesn't fit with the birth of Timothy who died September 15, 1891 at 1 year 15 days, giving him a birth date of August 31, 1890. In researching the 1900 census at the Mississippi Archives, I found that Eugenia was actually born in February 1900. Why the marker was wrong and why it was never corrected, no one knows.

5. WHWJr. we assume was William Hatton Williams, Jr. and was stillborn, and died when Gussie died in 1918.